"How do you f...
kissed in publ...

"I'd say, after hot fudge sundaes, it might become my next favorite thing," Lizbeth replied.

"Maybe we should do it again."

"One public kiss is all you get. Besides, you're melting my ice cream. I can't remember when I've had such a satisfying day. I wish it didn't have to end."

"It doesn't," Colin said.

Lizbeth knew her lips were quivering, and she hated that even now, after all these years, she could be moved by her memories. "If there's one thing I've learned, it's that nothing good lasts forever."

"If you believe that, then why not reach for whatever happiness you can today, and to hell with tomorrow?" He touched a hand to her cheek and leaned close. "You have to know that I want you, Lizbeth. Desperately."

"I know. And I want…" She wanted forever with this man, but she knew he wanted only tonight. Then again, couldn't forever start with a single glorious night?

Dear Reader,

Valentine's Day is here this month, and what better way to celebrate the spirit of romance than with six fabulous novels from Silhouette Intimate Moments? Kathleen Creighton's *The Awakening of Dr. Brown* is one of those emotional tours de force that will stay in your mind and your heart long after you've turned the last page. With talent like this, it's no wonder Kathleen has won so many awards for her writing. Join Ethan Brown and Joanna Dunn on their journey into the heart. You'll be glad you did.

A YEAR OF LOVING DANGEROUSLY continues with *Someone To Watch Over Her,* a suspenseful and sensuous Caribbean adventure by Margaret Watson. Award winner Marie Ferrarella adds another installment to her CHILDFINDERS INC. miniseries with *A Hero in Her Eyes,* a real page-turner of a romance. Meet the second of bestselling author Ruth Langan's THE SULLIVAN SISTERS in *Loving Lizbeth*—and look forward to third sister Celeste's appearance next month. Reader favorite Rebecca Daniels is finally back with *Rain Dance,* a gripping amnesia story. And finally, check out *Renegade Father* by RaeAnne Thayne, the stirring tale of an irresistible Native American hero and a lady rancher.

All six of this month's books are guaranteed to keep you turning pages long into the night, so don't miss a single one. And be sure to come back next month for more of the best and most exciting romantic reading around—right here in Silhouette Intimate Moments.

Enjoy!

Leslie J. Wainger
Executive Senior Editor

Please address questions and book requests to:
Silhouette Reader Service
U.S.: 3010 Walden Ave., P.O. Box 1325, Buffalo, NY 14269
Canadian: P.O. Box 609, Fort Erie, Ont. L2A 5X3

Loving Lizbeth
RUTH LANGAN

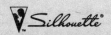
Silhouette®

INTIMATE MOMENTS™

Published by Silhouette Books

America's Publisher of Contemporary Romance

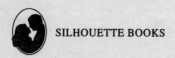 SILHOUETTE BOOKS

ISBN 0-373-27130-1

LOVING LIZBETH

Books by Ruth Langan

RUTH LANGAN

Award-winning and bestselling author Ruth Langan creates characters that *Affaire de Coeur* magazine has called "so incredibly human the reader will expect them to come over for tea." Four of Ruth's books have been finalists for the Romance Writers of America's (RWA) RITA Award. Over the years, she has given dozens of print, radio and TV interviews, including some for *Good Morning America* and *CNN News,* and has been quoted in such diverse publications as the *Wall Street Journal, Cosmopolitan* and the *Detroit Free Press.* Married to her childhood sweetheart, she has raised five children and lives in Michigan, the state where she was born and raised.

For Mary, our family whirlwind,
who does it all, and makes it look easy.

And for Tom, who taught her how.

Prologue

Dublin, Ireland—1982

"Grandpa Sully." Nine-year-old Lizbeth Sullivan's hazel eyes were damp with tears. Her sad voice was little more than a hushed whisper. "Why are Mom and Daddy sending me away to boarding school? Did I do something bad?"

"Don't be silly, LizzyBeth." Her grandfather used his pet name for his adored granddaughter as he drew her into the circle of his big arms. "They have to leave for Paris to start another hotel, and they worry that they'll be too busy to see to you and your sisters. It takes a lot of hard work and time to get a new business like ours up and running smoothly."

"But I could help. And so could Alex and Celeste." Lizbeth and her sisters always worked in the family hotels when they were home on holidays. It was not uncommon to see a ten-year-old standing on a ladder, washing windows. Or a nine-year-old in the kitchen, helping the salad chef. Or an eight-year-old dusting furniture.

Patrick Joseph Sullivan, who was called Paddy by his friends and Grandpa Sully by the three little girls who adored him, tousled her yellow curls. "I know you could help. And so could your sisters. But you can help even more by being good little girls and going off to school without a whimper. Can you do that, LizzyBeth?"

"But I'll miss you and Grandma. And Alex says we'll all be separated once we get to that fancy school. She'll be in class with the bigger girls. And Celeste will be in with younger ones. And I'll be..." Her lower lip quivered. "...all alone with strangers."

"Now, LizzyBeth, I taught you better than that. Come on now, lass. What's the Sullivan motto?"

She swallowed back her tears and lifted her chin. "At a Sullivan Inn, there are no strangers. Only people we have yet to meet."

"That's my girl. Now go pack your bags, luv. And when you kiss your parents goodbye, don't burden them with tears." He tipped up her chin. "Promise?"

"I...promise, Grandpa Sully."

She scampered up the stairs of the grand old hotel they currently called home. True to her word she held back her tears. But that didn't stop her from feeling the pain.

Oh, why couldn't they be a normal family like everybody else? With a house and a yard and neighbors? When she got old enough, Lizbeth vowed fiercely, that's what she would have. A lovely, cozy home, filled with all the things that had special meaning to her. And when she found such a place, she'd never ever leave it.

Chapter 1

Stafford, New Hampshire

Lizbeth Sullivan hated weeds. Especially weeds that sank their roots in her tidy vegetable garden. She'd spent the better part of an hour on her hands and knees in the dirt, pulling out the villains. Now, as she sat back on her heels, she felt a sense of satisfaction at the neat little rows of babies. She knew it was silly to think of beets and carrots and onions as her babies, but that's what they were. Along with the glorious peonies that had burst into bloom in a sunny spot alongside the white picket fence. Soon, as spring danced into summer, there would be lovely purple bearded irises, and a wonderful old climbing rose that produced hundreds of glossy white blooms each year.

Lizbeth loved each of the distinctive seasons here in the little town of Stafford, New Hampshire. But of all the seasons, spring was her favorite. With its warm days and chilly nights, and its often-fickle moods, there were few tourists. It meant, of course, that she had to be a bit more frugal until the arrival of summer, with its long, lazy days and endless string of vacationers in search of anything distinctly New England. Then the town of Stafford and her bed-and-breakfast, the cozy Stafford Cottage, would be filled to capacity. Though she would be busy from dawn until dark, it would be satisfying work. She loved sharing her home with the people who would come to her as strangers and leave as friends. There was an added bonus, of course. She would also be able to set aside enough profits to make the changes she was already planning on the east wing of the sprawling old house.

She could see it in her mind. If she could remove the walls between two of the smaller bedrooms, she could have her own master suite, equipped with a private sitting room and small office, apart from the rest of the house. It would give her the privacy she craved, while keeping her close enough to see to the many needs of her guests.

Though she was eager for the changes, she wasn't impatient. Anticipation, she realized, was

half the fun. Maybe that was why she loved springtime so much. While enjoying it, she could also
look forward to the season that followed.

She scooped up the last pile of weeds and tossed
them into the wheelbarrow. Getting to her feet, she
brushed a lock of hair from her eye before peeling
off her damp garden gloves.

A voice from behind had her turning around
abruptly.

"I'm looking for Lizbeth Sullivan."

The man facing her wore a faded denim jacket,
jeans and mud-caked work boots. He was tall
enough that she had to tip her head back to see his
face. It was worth the effort, since his eyes were
an incredible sparkling blue and his smile was as
warm as the sun. His cheeks and chin sprouted a
stubble of beard, adding a rough edge to his appearance. His dark hair curled damply, no doubt
from being tucked under the hard hat he held in
his hand.

"You've found her. I'm Lizbeth Sullivan."

He cocked a brow before offering a handshake.
"Colin St. James. Bill and Sue Yardley suggested
I might be able to rent a room from you while I
work on their place."

"You're handling the renovations on the Yardley house?"

"Yeah." His smile grew. "What a great old
place. I think I'm going to love working there."

He glanced around the tidy yard. "This looks great, too. Do you think you could put me up for the next month or two?"

"A month or two?" She knew her jaw dropped. She hoped he hadn't noticed as she carefully composed herself. But even as she thought how she would enjoy spending the money, she was mentally reminding herself that a laborer could hardly afford what she would be forced to charge. "That's going to be awfully expensive. Have you checked the motels outside of town? Some of them are fairly inexpensive, and might charge even less by the month."

He shook his head. "Not interested. This place is just too convenient to pass up. I could oversleep and still get to work on time."

"Do you do that often? Oversleep?"

His smile was quick and engaging. "Not as a rule. In fact, I'm an early bird. But I like this location. I'll be able to walk through the town and get a feel for the people and their surroundings. That's important when you're making major changes in a residence. Besides, my specialty is restoring antique buildings. I don't think I could stand to spend my nights staring at faded drapes and what passes for motel art on the bland walls."

Lizbeth couldn't help laughing. "I know what you mean. I suppose it's one reason why I love this old place. There isn't a bland wall to be found.''

It occurred to Colin that the proprietor wasn't bland either. He didn't know which was more beguiling. The way her hair had slipped loose of its combs to dip over one eye, or the smudge of dirt that stained her pretty pink cheek. In the sunlight her eyes were amber, ringed with a darker shade of honey.

The way he was staring at her sent a rush of unexpected heat curling along Lizbeth's spine. He had the most amazing eyes. So intense, they seemed to see clear through her.

Just then a man in a U.S. Postal uniform came whistling up the walk. ''Afternoon, Beth.'' He glanced at Colin, expecting an introduction.

''Jack Nowack, this is Colin St. James. He's going to be working at Bill and Sue Yardley's place.''

The mailman nodded a greeting to Colin. ''Heard they were going to start remodeling. Nice to meet you.''

He turned back to Lizbeth. ''Got a letter from your sister up in Snug Harbor. How're the newlyweds getting along?''

Lizbeth smiled as she accepted her mail. ''I'll read her note and let you know tomorrow, Jack.''

He touched the tip of his cap. ''Much obliged,

Beth. Nice meeting you, Colin. How long you think you'll be staying?''

Colin shrugged. ''Could be a month. Could be longer.''

''Good. You'll like it here in Stafford.'' The mailman started whistling as he walked away.

Lizbeth smiled. ''If you'll follow me, I'll give you a tour and you can decide if it's worth the fortune I intend to charge you to stay at Stafford Cottage.''

She lifted the wheelbarrow and pushed it to a small potting shed before leading the way to the back door, where she slipped out of her garden shoes before stepping inside. She was pleased to note that Colin St. James removed his work boots before following.

Inside, several loaves of date nut bread were cooling on a rack beside the stove. The kitchen was perfumed with the fragrance of them. Colin paused a moment to study the rainbow of light that spilled through a stained-glass panel above the sink and sent colors dancing across the hardwood floor.

The room was large enough to accommodate a huge table on which rested a marble slab. The kind used to cool fudge in an old-fashioned candy shop. In the center of the table was a low bowl of flowers. There were more flowers on the countertop and the windowsill.

Across the room a wood fire burned on the grate

of an enormous fireplace. A loveseat was positioned in front of it to absorb as much warmth as possible.

Lizbeth paused. "I need to wash up. If you follow that hallway, you'll find yourself in the main parlor."

"Thanks." Colin was still smiling as he ran a hand along the ornate wood molding that trimmed walls papered in shell-pink silk moire.

Minutes later he stood in the parlor admiring the ivory-inlaid desk that had to be at least two hundred years old.

He turned when Lizbeth entered. "This is a beautiful piece. Did it come with the house?"

She shook her head, pleased that he'd noticed it. "No. I found that in Maine, and had it shipped here. It cost way too much, but I simply couldn't resist."

"I can see why you had to have it."

Flushed with pleasure she took a seat and indicated the chair across from her. She'd taken those few minutes of privacy to figure out just how much she'd need to charge and still show a profit, while keeping the price low enough that Colin St. James would be able to take home a paycheck when his work here in Stafford was finished.

"In season I charge sixty-five dollars a night for a single. But since this is our off-season, and you've indicated that you might like to stay for a month or two, I think a thousand a month is a fair price. That's half the regular fee. That will include meals, of course. And the use of the laundry facilities.''

He nodded. ''That's more than fair.'' He pulled a credit card from his wallet and handed it to her.

She opened a guest book to a blank page and turned it toward him. ''Would you like to sign the guest register?''

She processed the credit card and handed it to him. When she glanced down, she noted the bold handwriting. It seemed to suit the man. At least what she'd seen of him so far.

''If you'd like to get your luggage, I'll show you to your room.''

A few minutes later she watched through the window as he strolled to his truck and lifted two huge suitcases as easily as if they weighed nothing at all.

Again he left his boots at the door before following her up the stairs. He gave an admiring glance at the grandfather clock on the landing, chiming out the half hour.

''What great chimes.''

She paused and nodded. ''It chimes on the half hour, and counts out the time on the hour. My Grandpa Sully gave it to me as a housewarming gift. It belonged to his father. He said he hoped it would remind me that time can be used wisely or foolishly. The wise person spends time pursuing those things that bring joy, and never wastes time dwelling on unhappiness.''

''Sounds like good advice.'' As he turned away Colin ran his hand along the mahogany handrail, worn smooth through the ages.

''Here you are.'' She stood back while he stepped inside.

His slow gaze took in the huge four-poster bed, covered in a warm burgundy plaid coverlet, and the wide window seats covered in the same fabric. Firewood was stacked neatly alongside the fireplace, with logs and kindling already in place on the grate.

''Are you sure you weren't expecting guests?''

She dimpled. ''In my business I have to be prepared. Will this suit your needs?''

He nodded, and she could see the pleasure in his eyes as he studied the mahogany Hepplewhite desk, the eighteenth-century armoire, the comfortable wing chair and ottoman, and beside it a table and reading lamp.

''The bath is equipped with both a shower and whirlpool tub.''

''I'm sure that didn't come with the house.''

She laughed. ''I had to add a few modern amenities if I wanted to keep my guests happy.''

''The whirlpool will come in handy after a day of heavy construction work.''

"Will you be doing the work yourself?"

"I'll have a crew. But I know I'll be working right alongside them. It's costing the Yardleys a lot of money to restore their house, and I intend to see that they get their money's worth."

"That's nice to hear. I know their family home means a lot to Bill and Sue. It's been in the Yardley family for almost two hundred years." She turned away. "I'll leave you to settle in. Dinner will be ready around six. But if you'd like to relax in the library, I'll have some nibbles and cocktails available. At the bottom of the stairs turn right. It will be the first door on your left."

When she was gone, Colin opened his first suitcase and began hanging clothes in the armoire. As he did, he couldn't help chuckling to himself. When Bill and Sue Yardley had recommended this place, he'd expected the proprietor to be a fussy old woman. It hadn't occurred to him that he might be spending the next month or more in the company of someone as fascinating as Lizbeth Sullivan.

He suddenly realized that not only was his work promising to be satisfying, but his off-hours might be equally challenging. He was definitely looking forward to his time spent in Stafford, New Hampshire.

Lizbeth put away her garden tools and disposed of the weeds, before making her way to her room where she showered and dressed. The arrival of a guest had just changed all her plans. Instead of a simple supper, she would now have to give consideration to something a bit more substantial.

She couldn't help smiling. In truth, she liked nothing better than preparing a meal for a man who enjoyed eating. And Colin St. James looked like just such a man.

In the kitchen she checked her supplies and decided on veal. While she prepared the marinade, she mentally assembled the rest of the menu. Garlic mashed potatoes, a lovely salad of spring greens. And rolls, freshly baked. She was humming as she sifted flour, measured baking powder, cut in shortening.

When she set the rolls to bake in the oven she made her way to the library, to check the bar. Satisfied that it was perfectly stocked, she filled a crystal bowl with ice and added tongs, then set a tray of crystal goblets beside it. As she returned to the kitchen she was already calculating how much time she had to fix a tray of appetizers.

She arranged finger-sized pastries filled with spinach and cheese, and paused to pop one in her mouth. The tourist season had arrived early this year in Stafford. And no one could be happier than she.

Thanks to Colin St. James, she would be a little bit closer to her dream of a master suite by this time next year.

* * *

Colin had no trouble finding the library. He paused in the doorway and looked around appreciatively. It was a cozy room, with floor-to-ceiling shelves, some displaying books, others framed with lovely old leaded-glass doors displaying treasures and photographs.

A fireplace added to the warm atmosphere. With its rose marble surround and a mantel of hand-carved teak, it offered an inviting spot to enjoy the eclectic collection of contemporary books and dog-eared classics.

Spotting the tray of appetizers, he walked closer and helped himself to one before pouring a tumbler of fine, aged Scotch. Glass in hand he inhaled the fragrance of fresh flowers as he began to circle the room, pausing to admire the video collection. Hearing Gershwin playing softly in the background, he located the CD player behind a cabinet door and discovered an amazing array of discs, from country to classical.

He sipped his Scotch and bent to a photograph showing three little girls standing on the balcony of what appeared to be a castle. His eye was drawn to the plump little blonde in the middle. It was undoubtedly Lizbeth Sullivan. The same unruly hair, curling around a face that looked both wise and serene. Though the other two looked very different, one with long straight honey-colored hair, the other with a short red bob, there was no question they were sisters. Behind them stood a man and woman, who looked very much as if they might own such an opulent home.

"My sisters, Alexandra and Celeste."

He turned. Lizbeth paused in the doorway, then crossed the room to stand beside him. She'd changed into a long flowered skirt that skimmed her ankles and a pink sweater trimmed at the collar and cuffs with the same flowered fabric. She'd scooped her hair up at her nape, leaving little tendrils loose to kiss her cheeks. The effect was both simple and elegant.

"And your parents?"

She nodded.

"Were you staying in a castle?"

"Yes. Castle Dunniefrey, just outside Dublin. My family owns it."

"They own it?" He gave her an incredulous look.

"It's been in the family for generations. When my Grandpa Sully…" She smiled. "Patrick Joseph Sullivan, went into the hotel business, he started by opening his family estate to the public."

He shook his head and laughed softly. "I should have known. But of course, I just hadn't connected you with those Sullivans. Why are you here when you could be running one of those five-star hotels in Europe?"

"I've done that. But in my travels I found Stafford Cottage, and fell in love. This is where I choose to be.''

She smelled like crushed roses, and he had the strangest urge to draw her close and breathe her in. Instead he held up his glass. ''Can I fix you a drink?''

''Yes, thank you. There's a bottle of chardonnay and a corkscrew beside it.''

He seemed reluctant to step away, but when he did, Lizbeth found herself taking two very calming breaths. She hadn't expected the man in faded denims and work boots to look so elegant. He'd shaved. And the face without the stubble was even more handsome. His charcoal slacks appeared to be custom-tailored. The gray crewneck was silk. And the loafers, worn without socks, were definitely Italian. The overall effect was devastating.

Within minutes he was back, holding out a stem glass of pale white wine. As she accepted it, their fingers brushed and he absorbed the most pleasant of sensations before she abruptly withdrew her hand.

He sipped his drink and took a step closer, aware that when he did, she took a step back. So she didn't like being crowded. By anyone? He wondered. Or just by him?

Interesting.

In fact, he thought, everything about this day had suddenly become extremely fascinating. This small town. This bed-and-breakfast. Its beautiful proprietor. If he'd thought the new job was a challenge, it was nothing compared with this.

Stafford, New Hampshire, it seemed, was about to get better and better.

Chapter 2

"Is this your grandmother?" Colin nodded toward another photograph of an elegant, white-haired woman embracing three younger women.

"Yes." Just looking at that photo made Lizbeth smile.

"That looks like the Square of St. Marks in Venice."

"You have a good eye. We were vacationing there the summer I finished my internship with Grandpa Sully at his hotel in Lake Como. Have you been to Venice?"

He nodded. "Several times. Part of my architectural training was spent studying the castles and great manor houses of Europe."

"You're an architect? I thought you were a building contractor."

"Both. With a specialty in restoration. There's probably much more money to be made in contemporary design, but my heart lies in restoring old buildings. I love the challenge of making them compatible with today's lifestyle, while finding a way to retain their charm." He pointed to the buildings in the background of the photo. "I admire the Europeans. They're experts at it. I've incorporated a lot of their ideas into my work."

At the sound of a buzzer Lizbeth looked up. "That's my kitchen timer. If you'll excuse me, I'll bring our dinner to the dining room." She paused in the doorway. "Just down the hall. Second door on your right."

Colin watched the way the skirt hugged her shapely backside, the hem dancing around her ankles as she turned away. She made such a pretty picture. Especially whenever a flush stole over her cheeks. Which happened whenever he looked at her a little too directly. It was sweet and endearing.

He finished his drink before making his way to the dining room.

It was a large room, which could easily accommodate twenty or more people. A highly polished Regency-style mahogany dining table, on which rested elegant crystal candlesticks, dominated the center of the room. To one side, in a bay window overlooking a garden abloom with peonies, a small round glass table had been set for two. It was so surprising and so perfect, Colin found himself smiling as he began to explore the room.

The hardwood floor was polished to a high sheen. Over that, directly under the table, was a beautiful rug in a colorful stained-glass design. Along two walls were shelves holding a collection of pitchers in jeweled tones that rivaled the brilliant colors in the rug.

Over an eighteenth-century Chippendale sideboard was a framed quilt that was equally bright and charming. It had been cleverly designed to resemble a Monet watercolor. Colin was still studying it when Lizbeth entered, pushing a serving cart filled with various covered dishes.

He nodded toward the open bottle of red wine on the side table. "Would you like me to pour?"

"Yes, thanks. That would be nice."

He was just setting down their wine glasses when she lifted the cover of a silver tray, releasing the wonderful steamy fragrance. "I hope you like veal."

Colin breathed in and felt his mouth water. "If it tastes half as good as it smells, I'm going to love it." He carried two glasses to the table, and took the seat Lizbeth indicated.

When their plates were served, she took her seat across from him and sipped her wine while Colin tasted the veal. She felt a flush of pleasure at his reaction. For a moment he closed his eyes, savoring the delicate taste.

"You marinated this in Marsala wine, right?"

She nodded.

"And a hint of something..." He tasted again. "Hmm. Lemon. Capers. This is sheer heaven."

"You know your way around a kitchen."

"A little."

She couldn't help smiling as she watched him devour his meal. Oh, she was going to enjoy feeding this man for however long he chose to stay.

"Do you grow your own vegetables?"

"As many as I can. It's early yet. But I've already been able to pick leaf lettuce and chard and little green onions." She sprinkled dressing on her salad and tasted. "I grow an herb garden year round in my kitchen. But I really like the bigger challenge of digging in the dirt and watching things grow from seed."

He glanced admiringly at the peonies outside the window. "I can see that you do. Your flowers seem to be flourishing. Is this where you eat when you're alone?"

She nodded. "I never grow tired of it. The scene changes with each new season."

He wondered if she knew how she looked when her eyes grew all soft and dreamy, and her dimples deepened. "You've created quite a home for yourself here.'' He glanced up at the colorful valance above the bay window. ''Did you make that?''

''Yes. And the rug under the table. And the quilt over the sideboard.'' She saw his look of surprise and felt a flush of pleasure. ''I love to sew. And quilt and knit and crochet. My grandmother taught me one summer, when my parents were off investigating another hotel. She knew I was missing them terribly, and so she contrived to fill my days. I'm sure she had no idea how much I would take to it. My two sisters had so many interests. Could do so many things. While my sister, Alex, was off exploring fields and streams, and Celeste was studying Shakespeare or taking in another art exhibit, I fell in love with homemaking.'' She colored. ''And here I am, all these years later, still amusing myself with simple things, while they're off pursuing all manner of fascinating things.''

''Don't put yourself down. It's a wonderful gift. And you've certainly created a home you can be proud of.'' He nodded toward the collection of pitchers. ''Yours?''

''Some of them belonged to my grandmother. She knew how much I loved them, and so she left them to me. Since then, I've added some of my own. Each one has a special meaning.'' She crossed the room and returned with a shimmering cobalt pitcher with a crystal stopper that seemed to catch the fading rays of sunlight and shoot sparks along the ceiling. "When I was a little girl this was my favorite. I remember weaving fanciful stories about a genie who lived inside, and would one day grant me whatever I wished for."

He reached for it and their hands touched. "So, have you dared to remove the stopper and let the genie loose?"

It occurred to her that his eyes were the same brilliant shade of blue as the pitcher.

She pulled herself back from the thought and managed a smile. "I guess I'll just have to wait until there's something I want badly enough to test the power of the genie."

He couldn't resist closing his hand over hers. He felt the way she started to draw away before he tightened his grasp and shot her a challenging smile. "I wouldn't wait too long if I were you."

"Why is that?"

"Genies live to make us happy. The poor guy's stuck in there snoozing when he'd rather be out here granting wishes."

"He'll get his chance." As she returned the pitcher to the shelf, it annoyed her to note that her hand was shaking slightly.

The first time Colin had touched her, in the library, she'd convinced herself she'd only imagined the heat. But it had just happened again. And this time there was no doubt in her mind. His simple touch had started a tingling in her fingers that had sizzled all the way up her arm.

She paused beside the serving cart. "More wine?"

He shook his head. "But if you're offering, I'll have a slice of that bread."

She handed him the plate and watched the way he tasted, sighed.

"My aunt used to make a date nut bread every Thanksgiving that we all loved so much, she would send a loaf to each family." He took another bite. "I think yours may be even better than aunt Betty's." He winked. "But if you quote me, I'll have to deny I ever said that."

Lizbeth couldn't help laughing. "Too bad I didn't have a tape recorder handy. I could have blackmailed you into paying a very nice bonus at the end of your stay here."

"I can see this could spell trouble. That's the last compliment you get from me." He polished off the bread, then sat back, sipping strong, hot coffee.

They sat together, watching as the first of the evening shadows began to flit across the garden. It occurred to Lizbeth that Colin might be hoping to end this meal so that he could join some of his working buddies for a drink at the local pub.

"Have you made plans for the evening?"

He shook his head. "I figured after the long drive here, I'd probably want to turn in early."

"Where did you come from?"

"Boston. That's where I finished my last renovation."

"And where is your home?"

He shrugged. "I have a loft in my office in Boston. I guess you could call that my home. But I really just live wherever I happen to be working."

"A true vagabond?"

"Yeah." He laughed. "It stems from my childhood. I was an Army brat. My sister, Serena, and I have lived all over the world."

"Where does she live now?"

"In Hawaii. But only temporarily. She and her husband, Gary Conyers, will be sailing to Fiji soon. He sells exotic boats. I think he knows everything there is to know about them. One of his clients has asked him to captain a yacht for the next year, with my sister going along as a member of the crew. Since they were both ready for their next great adventure, they agreed."

Lizbeth shook her head in wonder. "And after a lifetime of traveling, your sister has no desire to put down roots?"

Colin chuckled. "Serena would tell you that spending a year aboard a yacht is sinking roots. If she survives it, that'll be the longest she's ever lived in one place." He looked over at her. "How about you? Ever get an itch to pull up stakes and try your hand in some other place?''

''Not since I found this.'' She poured coffee for herself from an ornate silver pot and stirred in cream. ''I think I knew the moment I moved here that this was where I wanted to stay.''

''You're lucky.'' He studied her across the table, enjoying the way her hair had already slipped free of its combs to curl around her cheeks. She might keep a tidy house, but her hair, it seemed, had a will of its own. ''Some people spend a lifetime never finding a place where they belong.''

''Maybe they just haven't looked in the right places.'' She glanced up to find him staring at her. To cover her discomfort she asked, ''More coffee?''

''Yes.'' He reached for the pot at the same moment she did, and his fingers brushed hers before she pulled her hand back.

She could feel the heat staining her cheeks. To cover her awkwardness she got to her feet. ''Maybe you'd like to finish your coffee in the library. I have an excellent collection of books, movies and music.''

''Yeah. I noticed.''

''There's also some fine, old brandy, if you'd like an after dinner drink.''

''What about you?''

''I'm going to see to these dishes.'' As she began clearing the table and loading the serving cart she added, "You may even want to take a stroll around town before it grows too dark."

As she pushed the cart from the room he sat back a moment, watching her retreating back. Then he smiled to himself. If he wasn't mistaken, his lovely innkeeper was scheming to get rid of him. It would seem that he made her uncomfortable.

That thought made him all the more determined to find out why.

Lizbeth disposed of the cart in the kitchen, then returned to the dining room to wipe down the table. She was pleased to find the room empty. She didn't think she could take any more of those long, probing looks. Did Colin do that on purpose, she wondered, just to watch her squirm? Or was he unaware of what he was doing?

She mentally shook herself. Get over it, she cautioned. He was going to be here for a month or more. And she couldn't afford to freeze up every time the man looked at her.

He had the most incredible eyes. She paused in her work to glance out the window at the darkening sky. A deep midnight blue. And a killer smile. It was a good thing she was the calm, sensible type. Wasn't that what everyone said about her? Good old reliable Lizbeth. If she were anything else, she might have a tough time ignoring all that charm.

Annoyed with the direction of her thoughts she made her way back to the kitchen and began rinsing the dishes before loading the dishwasher. When the door opened she looked up to see Colin standing in the doorway. He strolled in carrying a bottle of brandy and two snifters, which he set on the counter.

She shot him a puzzled look. "Did you need something?"

"I thought I'd keep you company."

"I'm...just finishing up the dishes."

"Yeah. I can see that." He shot her a wicked smile. "My timing was perfect. I figured if I gave you a couple of minutes, you'd have most of them done."

He nodded toward the fireplace, where a cozy fire burned. "Want me to add another log?"

"If you don't mind."

He tossed a log on the fire, then poured brandy into two snifters. He lifted one between his hands, letting the warmth of his palms heat the liquid. And all the while he watched her.

She added detergent and set the dials before closing the door of the dishwasher. Then she wiped down the serving cart, and finally the counter and sink, before drying her hands.

Colin leaned a hip against the back of the loveseat. He liked watching her. He admired the economy of movement. The ease with which she managed the routine. Nothing hurried. Nothing careless. And he liked the way she looked in her kitchen. Comfortable, with herself and her surroundings. But what he liked best was simply the way she looked. That sweater and long sweep of skirt revealing a body that was all softness and curves. And that untidy mass of curls that made him itch to touch.

He watched as she began tying several loaves of date nut bread with a length of pretty ribbon. "A gift?"

"Yes." She kept her back to him as she finished. "Loretta Mayfair is my closest neighbor. She lives just down the street, beyond my garden. She's ninety-two and finds it hard to bake the things she once made. So whenever I bake something that I think she'd like, I always make extra for her. I'll take it to her tomorrow, along with a couple of little pots of jelly."

"Which you made, of course."

"Of course." She turned and found him grinning.

"Do you have anything more that needs to be done?"

She shook her head. "That's it for tonight."

"Good. Now you've earned the right to relax." He handed her a snifter of brandy and led the way toward the loveseat. "Why don't we sit over here?"

As they settled themselves, it occurred to Colin that she took great pains not to touch him. That only made him more determined than ever to find out why.

He fingered the afghan tossed carelessly over the back of the loveseat. It was as soft as an angel's wings. "Did you make this, too?"

She nodded. "It passes the time in the evenings." She tried not to shiver as his fingers brushed a strand of her hair before he released the afghan to pick up his snifter.

He smiled. "I'm sure I could think of plenty of ways to pass the time here." Especially with the woman sitting beside him. If she knew what he was thinking, those pretty little cheeks would be bright red.

He stretched out his feet toward the fire. "This is really nice. I bet you spend a lot of time here on cold winter nights."

"It's one of my favorite spots in the house. Though in truth I have so many favorites, it's hard to make a choice. I love my library. And there's a wonderful little attic room that I'm thinking of turning into a sewing room, so I can get some of the clutter out of my bedroom."

She sipped the brandy and sighed. How long had it been since she'd sat in front of the fire with a snifter of brandy? A year, at least. And even longer since she'd done so with a handsome man beside her. She glanced over. "How did you get the job with the Yardleys? Did you have to submit a bid?"

"No. A mutual friend recommended me. Bill and Sue drove up to Boston to see a sample of my work and hired me on the spot. I warned them it might take a while, since I was in the middle of a big project. But they were willing to wait." He held her gaze. "And now that I'm here, I'm glad they did. I wouldn't have missed this for the world."

"Then you like Stafford?"

"I like what I've seen so far."

He was doing it again. Staring at her the way a wolf might study a tasty lamb. To cover her nerves she stood and took a poker to the fire. "I hope you find time to explore the town. There are some really lovely old houses here. And the shops along Main Street aren't just for the tourists. There are several really grand restaurants. And The Village Pub does a lively business. It's where most of the townspeople go on a Friday night."

He set aside his snifter and stood. "Is that where you go, Lizbeth?"

"Not often. I prefer my own company." She set aside the poker and turned to find him standing directly beside her. She flushed. "Most people call me Beth. It's just simpler than Lizbeth."

He reached a hand to her hair, needing to touch it. It was as soft as he'd imagined it would be. Like fine gold silk. He twisted a strand around his finger. "I think I prefer Lizbeth."

He saw the way her eyes widened and knew she was poised to run. Before she could he brought his hands to her shoulders and lowered his face to hers. "It just suits you." He drew her closer. "Yes. Lizbeth definitely suits you." He could feel the little ripples of shock and distress as she started to pull back. And though he knew better, he found he couldn't resist brushing her lips with his.

It was the merest touch of mouth to mouth. But it had wings of fear beating furiously in her chest. She made a sound that might have been pleasure or protest.

He could taste her nerves. But he kept his eyes steady on hers. Kept his mouth on hers, unwilling to end the moment just yet.

She was wonderful to watch. The way her eyes widened, before her lashes fluttered, then closed. The way her pale skin became infused with color. The way her breath became a soft sigh that whispered over his senses, making him want to draw out the moment even longer.

There was such sweetness in her. It was a sweetness a man could get lost in if he wasn't very careful.

He changed the angle of the kiss, still keeping it light. Suddenly a need he hadn't expected caught him by surprise. A need to kiss her until they were both breathless.

Not a good idea, he realized. If he did, she'd run like a rabbit, and that wall of reserve would be even higher.

Reluctantly, he pulled back. The kiss ended as abruptly as it had begun.

His voice was rougher than he'd intended. "I'll say goodnight now, Lizbeth."

He saw the stunned look in her eyes before she composed herself.

"Good night."

As he climbed the stairs, he realized he was sweating. And his hands on the rail were none too steady.

What had just happened back there? It had started out as a whim, but had turned into something far different. A simple kiss had become something he wouldn't easily forget. And all because of the sweet, hypnotic pull of Lizbeth Sullivan.

Chapter 3

Lizbeth squeezed orange juice and filled a crystal pitcher before placing it on a tray alongside the fresh fruit compote she'd assembled in a lovely ceramic bowl. Then she ground coffee beans and started the coffee maker, before opening the oven, where fresh biscuits were perfectly browned. Eggs sizzled on the stove, and crisp bacon drained on a paper towel.

She was grateful for the work. It kept her from thinking, something she'd done too much of as she'd tossed and turned all night.

What was wrong with her? Why had she permitted a simple kiss to become this earth-shattering event? It was, to her way of thinking, further proof of how pathetic her existence had become. She was twenty-eight years old. Twenty-eight, for heaven's sake. And she could count the number of times she'd been kissed by a man.

But none of them had ever been like that kiss last night. It had been much more than a kiss. To her way of thinking, a fall from a bridge into frigid water would have been less shocking. She'd been absolutely paralyzed. And after Colin had left, she'd been numb. Too numb to do more than sink down onto the loveseat and stare blindly at the fire, wondering if she'd imagined the entire thing.

She paused. Her imagination wasn't wild enough to have conjured such feelings. She'd been hot and cold and absolutely trembling. And all from a single kiss that had barely lasted more than a few seconds.

She shook her head. Pathetic. But there it was. One kiss and she was reduced to the whims of raging teen hormones. What stung even more was the fact that Colin had been as cool as if he'd done nothing more than shake her hand.

This was a new day, she reminded herself. A fresh start. And this time she'd act her age. She was almost thirty, a woman on her own for a long time now. If she could make her own way in the world, she could certainly deal with one handsome, charming guest who was probably indulging himself in nothing more than a harmless flirtation.

She heard Colin's footfall on the stairs and loaded breakfast on the serving cart before heading toward the dining room.

"Good morning." She breezed into the room and busied herself transferring the food from the cart to the table, proud of the fact that she'd given him barely a glance. But it had been enough to reveal that hard, muscled body she'd felt pressed to hers last night, encased in a flannel shirt and jeans. Why did he have to look so...potently male?

"Morning." He paused in the doorway and watched as she poured juice and coffee.

She looked as fresh as the morning sunshine in a crisp yellow blouse and slim, ankle-length denim skirt. Her hair was held off her face with combs that were almost lost in a tumble of curls.

She kept her face averted. "I hope you found your room comfortable."

"Yeah. Thanks." He moved closer and breathed her in. She smelled like a flower garden after a spring rain.

"There are two newspapers available." She lifted them from the serving cart and placed them beside his plate. "Our Stafford paper and a national newspaper, in case you don't care for local news."

"Now what makes you think I wouldn't care about local news?"

She shrugged, still avoiding his eyes. "Not much happens in a town like Stafford."

"Really? Is that why you chose to settle here?"

Stung by the truth she swiveled her head to find him watching her. She could feel the flush rising to her cheeks and cursed the fair skin that always seemed to give away her feelings. "I suppose that was part of its charm."

He merely smiled before taking his seat.

When she uncovered a plate of bacon and eggs and cottage-fried potatoes, as well a basket of perfectly browned toast and biscuits, his smile grew. "You do know how to feed a guy, Lizbeth Sullivan."

"I'm glad you approve. I figured, since you'll be doing hard, physical work, you'll want to start with something substantial."

He dug in. After a moment he glanced up. "Aren't you eating?"

She poured herself coffee. "I'm just having a biscuit and jam. I'll have a mid-morning snack with my neighbor when I bring her the date nut bread."

He glanced out the window. "Looks like it's going to be a great day. I'm glad it isn't raining. I plan to climb up on the Yardleys' roof and have a look before I get my crew started."

"The roof?" She blanched, imagining how her

heart would pound if she had to face such a daunting task.

"It's not so bad. I've worked on buildings ten times as high. If you're working, you never think about the height."

"Maybe you don't. I would never be so busy that I could forget I was on someone's roof."

He chuckled. "Well, if it makes you feel better, I'll admit that I prefer to do my work indoors. With floors under my feet and walls around me. But I've spent plenty of time crawling around attics, through basements, over roofs. Whatever it takes to get the job done."

He polished off the last of his eggs and sat back, draining his coffee. "This was a great workingman's breakfast. I think I'm ready to tackle the day now."

"I'm glad you enjoyed it."

When he pushed away from the table Lizbeth retrieved a thermal packet from the serving cart and handed it to him.

He arched a brow. "What's this?"

"Your lunch." She saw the quirk of his lips and said primly, "You're paying for your meals. I expect after a morning of crawling around the Yardleys' attic, roof and basement, you'll be glad to have it."

"Thanks. I'm not ungrateful. It's just that I wasn't expecting this kind of service."

"There's more." She handed him a thermal coffee dispenser.

At his look she said, "Whenever I've had workmen here, they always seem to drink gallons of coffee. I figure you'll go through this before noon."

He grinned. "You're going to spoil me." He tucked it under his arm as he headed for the door.

She saw him pick up a pair of work boots and carry them to the back door. Once outside, he paused to put them on before heading for his truck.

As he drove away she took a deep, calming breath and congratulated herself. She thought that had gone quite well.

Then, as she went about cleaning up the breakfast dishes, she gave herself a good talking to. She was going to have to stop reacting like a schoolgirl every time Colin came near. She paused to hold out her hands. They were trembling. And her palms were sweating.

She shook her head and began to laugh as she pushed the serving cart toward the kitchen. She really did need to find something challenging to occupy her mind. Otherwise, she was apt to replay that kiss a hundred more times. Something she definitely couldn't afford to do if she wanted to accomplish anything this day.

Colin unhooked his tool belt and made his way to his truck. The crew had been gone for almost an hour, but he'd lingered, making some sketches of the latest changes the Yardleys had requested. He wasn't surprised by the newest changes. Most people had an idea of what they wanted when they hired an architect. But once they saw the possibilities, they often came up with half a dozen more things they couldn't live without.

As he settled himself in the driver's seat he paused to study the house. It had the solid, sturdy feel of New England, with a high-pitched roof topped by an ancient weathervane. There had been additions to it through the years. A bedroom here, a library there. An entire wing had been added a generation ago. And the upper floor which had once been a large, dormitory bedroom was now an office shared by both Bill and Sue, who were graphic artists. But it had lost some of its style, becoming a hodgepodge of rooms and rooflines that needed to be pulled together into one cohesive unit.

Colin turned the key and drove along the graceful sweep of circular driveway. As the truck slowly traversed the short block to the Stafford Cottage, he drank in the sights and sounds of the small town.

A young mother pushed a stroller while a toddler on a tricycle pumped his little legs furiously to keep pace beside her. A girl of about thirteen took advantage of the sunshine to walk a fluffy white dog on a leash, while two teenage boys who'd been shooting hoops paused to watch admiringly. Some things never changed, Colin thought with a grin.

As he reached the end of the lane he turned into the driveway of Stafford Cottage and climbed down from his truck. He paused at the back door to remove his work boots, and halted when he heard a voice.

Peering around the back of the house he saw Lizbeth removing sheets from a clothesline. It looked like a scene from another era. Colin found himself staring as avidly as those teenage boys. She made quite a picture. Hair the color of moonbeams danced in the breeze and kissed her cheeks. The hem of her skirt fluttered and her blouse pulled free of her waistband as she reached for yet another billowing sheet. While she folded it into a huge wicker basket she carried on a conversation with a fat cat curled along the top rail of the fence.

"You're glad to see the sun, aren't you, Brandi? I bet you were giving Loretta all kinds of grief during our spell of rain last week."

She dropped the pins in her pocket and placed the last carefully folded sheet into the basket. Then she walked over to the fence to pick up the purring cat and bury her face in its fur. "I've missed you, you old rascal. I'm so happy you stopped by to visit. I get worried when I don't see you for a while. The same way I worry over Loretta. I'm glad you two have each other. Nobody should be alone.''

Colin wondered if he'd only imagined the wistful note in her voice.

She placed the cat back on the fence rail, then lifted the basket. When she turned, she saw Colin and hesitated before moving toward him.

''I didn't hear you drive in.''

''You were too busy talking to your visitor.''

She laughed. ''That's old Brandi. She's close to twenty now. But she can still make it to the top of the fence. Though I suspect her eyesight isn't what it once was.''

''Does she live with your elderly neighbor, Loretta?''

''She does.'' Lizbeth laughed. ''And if Loretta heard you call her elderly, she'd take a broom to you the same way she does to Brandi when that little scamp knocks over the flowerpots.''

''I'll keep that in mind.'' He reached for the basket. ''I'll take that.''

''It isn't heavy. Just bulky.'' But after a weak protest she relinquished it and walked along beside him. At the back door she held it open while he carried the basket of linens inside and set it atop the dryer.

"Isn't it a lot of work to hang these when you have a clothes dryer?"

She shrugged. "It may be a bit more work, but it's worth it. There's just something about the springtime. Everything smells so good."

He bent close to the basket and inhaled, then nodded. "Yeah. They smell like…"

"Like spring," she finished for him.

Though he nodded, he realized that what he'd really meant was that they smelled like her. So fresh and clean he wanted to keep on breathing her in until he was filled with her scent. Instead, he turned away. "Guess I'd better shower before dinner."

When he walked away Lizbeth began stacking the sheets. She'd managed to stay busy all day, without thinking about him once. Well, she corrected, maybe twice. Then, because she couldn't lie even to herself, she had to admit that she'd thought about him at least half a dozen times. But the image in her mind wasn't nearly as potent as the one she'd seen when she'd turned and found him watching her just now in the yard. He looked so pleased from a day of satisfying work. Dark hair mussed. Clothes damp and sweaty and plastered to him. A growth of five o'clock shadow on his lower face that only added to his charm. And that probing stare guaranteed to make a woman shiver.

She carried the folded sheets upstairs. As she

passed Colin's room she heard the stereo playing, and heard him singing above the sound of running water. She stored the clean sheets in the linen closet and turned away. As she descended the stairs she found herself smiling and humming along.

She couldn't remember the last time she'd heard the sound of a man singing in the shower in Stafford Cottage.

Colin made his way to the library and poured himself a drink. Tonight the music playing softly was classical. He recognized Beethoven's Ode to Joy. He thought about starting a book, and scanned the titles, looking for a good thriller. But though the shelves were stocked with several he'd been meaning to read, he found himself restless, turning often toward the door, hoping to see Lizbeth. When she didn't appear, he picked up his tumbler and made his way to the kitchen.

She was just setting a covered platter on the serving cart. She looked up in surprise. "I'm sorry. I'll bet you're hungry."

"No. I just wondered if you were going to join me in the library."

"Oh." She smiled. "I thought you might like some time alone to unwind after a day of work."

"What I really want is company." He held up his tumbler. "Would you like something to drink before dinner?"

She started to refuse, then thought better about it. "All right. There's some wine chilling in the dining room. If you'd like to open it, I'll have a glass."

He returned within minutes and handed her a glass of white wine.

While she sipped he looked around. There was a pleasant clutter to the kitchen. A roasting pan soaking in the sink. Cruets of oil and vinegar standing beside a salad bowl. A carving knife and long-handled fork, as well as a pair of oven mitts.

"Looks like you've been busy."

"Yes. Well…" She wished he wouldn't stand so close. It made thinking difficult. "I had a visit with Loretta Mayfair. Since she doesn't get out much, I had to fill her in on the latest town news. Then I took her shopping list along since I was heading to the village market. When I delivered her groceries and put them away, she insisted I stay for tea. That set me back a bit, but I know how much it means to her to have company, so I stayed as long as I could. Then I worked in my garden and did the laundry."

"And on top of all that, you had to make dinner."

She smiled. "Dinner is the easy part. I love to cook."

"It shows. I think you should know that the lunch you sent made me the envy of all my crew."

"Really?"

He could see the flush of pleasure on her cheeks. He had an almost irresistible desire to lean close and press a kiss to the spot. Instead he tightened his hand on his drink. "Yeah. The rest of them had to settle for fast food. It didn't come close to those roast beef sandwiches on home-baked bread, or the little container of pasta salad. I only got to eat two of those ginger cookies. The rest were devoured by my crew before I could stop them. I ought to warn you. They're taking bets on what I'll bring tomorrow. And figuring out how to get it away from me."

She laughed. "I think you're exaggerating. I wasn't sure what you liked, so I had to imagine what a hardworking man would want."

"Then you have an excellent imagination, Lizbeth."

If he only knew what that imagination had been doing to her all day.

When the buzzer sounded on the stove, she was relieved to move away. Just standing close to him had her uneasy.

She lifted the roasting pan from the oven and called over her shoulder, "If you'd like to pour yourself some wine, I'll serve in the dining room in a few minutes."

She noticed that he was smiling broadly as he

walked away, and had the feeling that once again he'd read her mind.

"I think maybe I ought to be concerned." Colin set aside his napkin and refused a second slice of apple pie.

"About what?" Lizbeth looked up from the serving cart where she was loading dishes.

"I've eaten more in two days than I usually eat in a week. At this rate, by the time I leave Stafford, I may have to ride in the back of my truck."

She laughed. "I wouldn't worry. With your job, I'm sure you'll manage to work it off."

As she started out of the dining room he surprised her by trailing along. At her questioning look he merely smiled. "I thought I'd start working it off right now."

When he opened the dishwasher she lifted a hand to stop him. "Wait, Colin. You can't do that."

"Why not?"

"You should be in the library reading or relaxing, not working. You're a paying guest."

"All the more reason to indulge me, Lizbeth. I don't want to read a book, or watch television or a video. I'd much prefer the pleasure of your company here in the kitchen."

"All right, then. Have a second cup of coffee while I do my work."

"Sorry." He began loading the dishwasher. "It's really all your fault. You make this look like such fun I feel like I'm missing out on something." He shot her a wicked smile as she began to wrap the leftovers. "I hope you saved enough of that roasted chicken for tomorrow's lunch."

She couldn't help laughing. "There's more than enough."

With the two of them working together the kitchen chores were done in no time. When Lizbeth finished putting away the last pan, she turned to find Colin holding two glasses of wine.

"There seemed no point in saving this." As he handed her a stem glass, he felt the warmth of her touch. "I noticed a glider on the front porch. As long as it's so mild out tonight, why don't we sit out there?"

They walked along the hallway, past the parlor, to the front door. Colin held the door and Lizbeth led the way across the porch to the glider.

As they settled side by side, he breathed deeply. The spring air was heavy with the perfume of peonies and lilacs. "Oh, this is nice."

"It is, isn't it?" She sipped her wine, then lifted her gaze to the inky sky, awash with millions of glittering stars. "I remember my Grandpa Sully telling me that that star—" she pointed "—the one at the tip of the handle of the Big Dipper, was his star. If I ever wanted anything, all I had to do was look up, find that star and make a wish, and he would tip that dipper my way and spill all my wishes into my lap.''

''Sounds like a very generous grandfather.''

''He is. He'd give my sisters and me the moon if he could.'' Lizbeth chuckled, remembering. ''He used to say that he knew what we wanted even before we did. And more often than not, he was right. It's odd. I'd settled nicely into the routine of managing one hotel after another, and I knew he was pleased with my work. But out of the blue he sent me here to New Hampshire to check out a hotel he wanted to buy for our chain. That's when I happened upon this cottage and fell in love with it. Until that moment I hadn't even known how weary I was of traveling the world. But I knew instantly that I wanted to sink down roots here. I've always wondered if Grandpa Sully had a hand in it, or if it was simply fate.'' She sighed. ''I suppose I'll never know. But knowing my grandfather, he'll manage to take the credit.''

Colin's hand was along the back of the glider. He could feel the brush of her hair. It seemed the most natural thing in the world to twine a curl around his finger. ''He must love you a lot.''

She could feel him playing with the ends of her hair. She wondered if he knew what that did to her nerves. ''He does.''

''I can see why.''

At the gruffness of his voice she turned to find his face so close to hers she could feel the warmth of his breath on her cheek.

"Don't, Colin."

Her eyes were wide. He could see the glint of starlight reflected in them. It made her even more enticing. "Don't what?"

"Don't kiss me."

He heard the way her voice trembled slightly. "You know I want to."

"I know. But I'm not…ready."

She could feel the tension humming through him. Could almost sense the way he mulled it over in his mind.

"All right." He drained his wine to soothe his dry throat. Then he touched a hand to her cheek before he drew it away and got to his feet. "Good night, Lizbeth."

"Good night."

She stayed where she was, listening as he crossed the porch and let himself in the front door.

As the silence of the night closed in around her, she realized that though he'd given in to her request without an argument, there was no sense of satisfaction. She ought to feel relieved. Instead, she felt oddly deflated.

She had her wish. And she found herself, as always, alone.

She leaned her head back and stared at the stars, fighting unexpected tears.

Chapter 4

Lizbeth latched the gate behind her and started up the street. She'd meant to get an earlier start, but her visit with her neighbor, Loretta, had taken considerably longer than she'd expected.

She closed her hand around the piece of paper in her pocket. It contained a list of errands she was determined to complete before dinner.

She liked lists. Liked being able to cross off items, as they were completed. It gave her a sense of satisfaction. A sense of accomplishment. It was probably what made her so good at operating a bed-and-breakfast. No matter how many guests filled her rooms, she was able to manage the food, the laundry, the cleaning and all the little extras that went into making their stay as luxurious as possible.

It was one of those near-perfect spring days. Though there was still a bite in the air, the sunshine made the day seem warmer. A fresh breeze caught tendrils of her hair, yanking curls from the combs anchoring them and whipping them around her cheeks. The hem of her spring-green skirt stopped just shy of her ankles, and was slit on either side to her knee to allow for walking. The breeze teased it with each step. The short-cropped yellow cardigan was just warm enough to fight the chill when she passed beneath the awnings of the shops along Main Street.

On a whim she veered from her path and followed the street that meandered into the residential section of town. For a week now Colin had been talking about the work he was doing at the Yardley house. She wanted to see for herself.

Even before the house and yard came into view she could hear the whine of an electric saw and the steady sound of hammering. When she reached the curving driveway, she stopped and lifted a hand to her forehead to shield the sun from her eyes. She was startled to hear her name.

"Beth." Sue Yardley waved a hand. "Come on in and see what we're up to."

"All right." Lizbeth started up the drive, aware that Colin was standing on the front porch with

Bill Yardley. Both men turned to watch her. "Just for a minute. I don't want to keep you from whatever you were doing."

"We were just showing Colin what we wanted to change here at the front entrance." Sue Yardley met her halfway and tucked her arm through Lizbeth's. "Bill and I seem to have a new idea every day."

"Hello, Beth." When they reached the top step Bill Yardley leaned over to brush a kiss on Lizbeth's cheek.

While she returned his greeting, she could feel Colin watching her.

Bill Yardley slapped Colin's arm. "We're so glad you were able to put this guy up at your place, Beth. He's a miracle worker. Wait till you see what he's doing with this old place."

Bill led the way inside, with the others trailing. Colin lagged slightly behind, enjoying the way Lizbeth looked, her cheeks pink, her hair mussed. He itched to touch her. Instead, he kept his hands tucked into his back pockets.

Just past the entrance foyer, a drop cloth covered the hall floor, and an entire wall was gone. Several workmen were busy drilling, sawing, hammering.

Bill Yardley had to shout over the noise. "When Colin's finished in here, we'll have a great room big enough to accommodate our family without spilling out into the dining room and kitchen."

Sue Yardley sounded ecstatic. "You know what our Fourth of July parties are like." She turned to Colin. "Who would know better? I always ask Beth to do most of the cooking. Now that you've had a sample, I'm sure you understand why."

He nodded, but before he could get a word in she went on in that same breathless voice, "Of course he knows. I've seen the lunches you've been packing for him. Makes the rest of his crew crazy when they're stuck with fast food, or whatever I can scrape up." Without a pause she said, "Won't it be grand when Bill and I can put up the whole family in here without feeling like sardines?"

Lizbeth nodded. "You're going to love it, Sue."

"Now you have to see this." Taking advantage of his wife's break in the conversation Bill led the way to another room, where carpet had been rolled back to reveal beautiful hardwood floors. "Look." He pointed. "We had no idea we had such hidden treasures. It took Colin to unearth it."

Lizbeth turned to him. "How did you know what you'd find?"

"Just an educated guess. Most of these old homes have all kinds of treasures that have been covered up through the ages. Usually it starts with a fad. Wall-to-wall carpeting that everyone has to have. Or wallpaper that is pasted over wonderful old coved ceilings. When you start paring down, you either find trash or treasure.''

"In our case it's all been pure gold so far." Sue Yardley squeezed her husband's hand. "We just couldn't be happier."

She turned to Lizbeth. "You really ought to consider keeping Colin on when he's through with our place so he could start on your renovations."

Colin shot her a quizzical look. "You're thinking of making some changes?"

She shrugged. "Just a few walls I thought I'd like to take down. Nothing as major as this."

"You'll have to show me some time."

She nodded. "All right."

It occurred to her that the house had grown quiet. Could the workmen be finished for the day?

"Oh, Beth. You haven't seen our other addition." Sue steered her into a cozy back room where a fat white-and-black cat lay in a basket. Climbing over the cat and spilling onto the floor were half a dozen tiny balls of fluff.

"Oh, Sue. Millie had her kittens." Lizbeth dropped to her knees and began petting them. At once they all began vying for her attention, struggling to climb into her lap, nipping at her finger.

Bill exchanged a glance with his wife. "I wish we could talk you into taking one of them home with you when they're old enough. We need to find them all loving homes."

Lizbeth was already getting to her feet, shaking down her skirts. "You know better than to ask, Bill."

"Yeah. So you've told me. But just because your last attempt at a pet failed is no reason not to try again."

"It's reason enough for me. I cried over that lost kitten for weeks."

Bill glanced at his watch. "We promised Bill Jr. we'd make it to his game, Sue. We'd better go."

He shook hands with Colin and brushed another kiss over Lizbeth's cheek before turning away.

Sue caught Lizbeth's hands. "Promise you'll come back in a few weeks and see the results of all Colin's work."

"I promise. I wouldn't miss it."

When the two were gone Lizbeth started to turn away. "I'm really sorry. I never meant to keep you from your work this long."

Colin unhooked his tool belt. "I was finished for the day. We were just going over a few more changes." He caught up with her in the doorway. "Come on. I'll drive you home."

"I have some stops to make first. Some errands I promised to run for Loretta."

"That's not a problem." He placed a hand beneath her elbow and moved out the front door and down the steps toward his truck.

When he held the door she had no choice but to

climb inside. As he came around and settled himself beside her she was still apologizing. "You don't understand. I have a lot of stops to make. You could be an hour or more waiting for me when you could be relaxing in your room."

"There's plenty of time to relax later." He turned the key and gave her a smile. "Where to first?"

She pointed. "Turn right here and another right at the end of the street. I'd better fill Loretta's prescription first."

They parked in front of the small village drugstore. Instead of waiting in the truck Colin surprised Lizbeth by going inside with her.

"Afternoon, Beth," came a voice from behind the counter.

"Hello, Seth. Seth Simpson, I'd like you to meet Colin St. James."

As the two men shook hands the druggist said, "I heard you were renovating the Yardley place. Staying at the Stafford Cottage, are you?"

"That's right."

"Not a finer place in Stafford than Beth's cottage." The druggist turned to her with a smile. "What can I do for you, Beth?"

"I have a prescription for Loretta." Lizbeth handed over the slip of paper.

He read it, then nodded. "It'll take a couple of minutes. She told me to expect you."

"She phoned you?"

"Yep. With a list of things she'd thought of after you left. I already have them ready right here." He lifted a bulging sack from beneath the counter.

Lizbeth laughed. "I guess I shouldn't be surprised."

She was still smiling as he walked away, returning minutes later with a small bottle of tablets which he placed in the sack.

She withdrew a check from her pocket. "Loretta gave me a blank check and told me to fill in the amount."

"That'll be $37.65."

She filled in the numbers, then dropped the receipt in the sack. "Thanks, Seth. I guess I'll see you in a week or so."

"You have a good one, Beth. And you, too, Mr. St. James."

"Colin."

The older man nodded. "Colin. You come back again."

Before she could lift the sack, Colin picked it up and carried it to the truck. When it was stashed inside he turned to her. "Now where?"

"I need to pick up Loretta's cleaning. It's just two doors down. And then stop at The Village Market, which is just across the street."

He walked beside her, enjoying the fading sunshine. Inside the cleaners the girl behind the

counter looked up from her paperback novel.
"Hey, Beth."

"Amy. How's your mother?"

"Healing nicely." The girl stared pointedly at
Colin. "You must be the architect. I heard you
were staying at the Cottage."

"That's right. Colin St. James." He offered his
hand.

She wiped her hand on her jeans before tenta-
tively offering her handshake. "Amy Mullins."

"Amy's been helping out after school since her
mom started chemotherapy."

"She really appreciated the meals you sent over
for us, Beth. Even though she couldn't eat most of
them."

"Is she feeling stronger now?"

"Yeah. She had the last chemo two weeks ago,
and swears her appetite is finally coming back."

"Oh, I'm so glad, Amy. If she's up to having
visitors, I'll stop by next week."

"She'd like that." The girl smiled. "You picking up Loretta's cleaning again?"

"Yes. Is it ready?"

Amy nodded and walked into a back room, returning minutes later with several garments in plas-
tic bags. "Every year Loretta sends her best dress
to be cleaned in time for the Spring Fling. You
know how fussy she is."

With a nod Lizbeth dug into her pocket and

handed over a handful of crumpled bills. Before she could pick up the cleaning, Colin took it and held the door.

As she started to follow, Amy caught her arm and muttered, "If I had someone like that staying at my place, I'd have better things to do than pick up Loretta Mayfair's cleaning."

"Amy. Hush." At the grin on Colin's lips Lizbeth could feel herself blushing all the way to her toes.

She waited while he hung the cleaning in the truck, then she led the way across the street to The Village Market. Inside she saw several heads turn as Colin separated a cart and began pushing it alongside her. She dug out her list and began to fill the cart. By the time they made it to the cashier, they'd been stopped more than a dozen times for greetings and introductions.

"Hi, Beth. Thanks for the donation to our church supper."

"Beth. I've been meaning to ask you for your recipe for that hot crab dip you made for our holiday party. Think you could write it down for me?"

"Beth. The women's club loves your idea of having local businesses donate planters which we can arrange all along Main Street. The town will look so pretty. Would you help us chair a committee?"

Colin shot her a sideways glance. "Sounds like they keep you hopping."

She gave an embarrassed laugh. "I don't mind. It's my town. I like being involved."

Two white-haired women in identical neon-yellow jogging suits paused and looked Colin up and down before turning to Lizbeth.

"Sister said you had an out-of-season border," the first woman said.

The second nodded. "Are you bringing him to the Spring Fling?"

"I..." Lizbeth could feel the heat starting up her throat and spreading over her cheeks. "I...hadn't thought about it."

They turned to Colin.

The first woman asked in imperious tones, "Do you dance, young man?"

"I don't embarrass myself on the dance floor."

"Our town is holding its Spring Fling next weekend. See that you bring Beth."

The second woman added, "And see that she dances this year, instead of hiding behind the dessert table."

When they walked away Lizbeth huffed a breath. "Just ignore those two busybodies. Alfreda and Winifred Lassiter make it their business to know everybody else's."

Colin was trying to keep a straight face. But it was a struggle. "I don't know. The Spring Fling doesn't sound so bad. Don't you know how to dance?''

"Of course I can dance."

"Then why do you hide behind the dessert table?''

"I don't hide. The desserts are my responsibility."

"Isn't there anyone who can help you?''

"There's Loretta. And Reverend Watson's wife, Mary Lyn.''

"I'd think they wouldn't mind if you took time for a dance or two.''

"Why are we talking about this when you haven't even said you were going?''

He grinned. "You haven't invited me yet.''

She reached for a box of oatmeal in silence.

"Hey, Beth." The woman at the register stared pointedly at Colin as she began mechanically ringing up the items. "I heard you had an out-of-season guest at the Cottage.''

"That's right, Vicky. Colin St. James, this is Vicky Carter.''

Colin nodded as he continued unloading the cart.

"Doing Loretta's shopping again?" Vicky asked.

Colin glanced up at Lizbeth. "How did she know?''

"The cat food, for one," Vicky said before Lizbeth could say a word. "And the oatmeal. I'd know Loretta Mayfair's groceries anywhere."

Colin had to hold back the rumble of laughter that threatened. Only in a town as small as Stafford would a cashier know an absent shopper by her groceries.

Vicky picked up the package of chocolate bars. "What's this? I know Loretta wouldn't order these."

Lizbeth grinned. "Those are my surprise for her. She has a sweet tooth."

"I should have known. What else are you buying out of your own pocket?"

Lizbeth looked embarrassed. "It doesn't matter, Vicky. Just ring them up."

When the woman had totaled the sale and accepted her money, she handed her back the change and said to Colin, "She does this every time. You'd think by now Loretta would figure out that she was getting more than she paid for."

"Thanks, Vicky." Still blushing, Lizbeth picked up a bag before Colin could beat her to it.

He picked up the other one and followed her from the store.

In the truck they stored the bags and started home. Just beyond Stafford Cottage was a vacant lot abloom with wildflowers, and then a small cottage that looked almost like a doll house.

"This is Loretta's place."

Their arms loaded with sacks and cleaning, they followed an overgrown path carved among a riot of flowers until they reached the porch. Lizbeth knocked and waited. After nearly five minutes, the door was opened and a stooped woman leaning on a cane greeted Lizbeth.

"My, you're back already. That was fast."

"I had help." Lizbeth stepped in and said, "Loretta, this is Colin St. James. The boarder I told you about."

Colin found himself being appraised by the sharpest blackbird eyes he'd ever seen. At his feet the cat Brandi was busy making figure eights.

"Hello, Mrs. Mayfair."

"It's Loretta."

"Loretta." He gave her a smile, then bent to scratch behind Brandi's ears.

The old woman admonished, "Careful. She'll bite. She doesn't like strangers. Especially men."

No sooner were the words out of her mouth than the cat arched herself against his hand and began purring.

Colin granted her several long, smooth strokes along her back before straightening. "Where would you like these, Loretta?"

"Straight through that doorway. You can set them on the kitchen table. Beth knows where everything goes."

She shuffled behind him. When she reached the

kitchen she caught hold of the back of a chair, while her cat leapt up on the counter and waited for the expected treat. She wasn't disappointed when Lizbeth opened a can of cat food and spooned it into a dish.

Loretta caught sight of the bag of chocolates. "I didn't order those, Beth."

"You didn't?" Lizbeth shrugged. "I would have sworn I read chocolate on your list."

Loretta's tone was sharp. "I hope you didn't lose the receipt again."

Lizbeth flushed and began to dig through her pockets. "It's here somewhere, Loretta. I'll find it after I put away your food."

While Lizbeth stashed the groceries, the old woman stood assessing Colin.

"Beth says you're remodeling the Yardley place."

"That's right."

"You're the architect?"

He nodded. "And the builder."

"So, you work with your hands and your mind."

"That's a good way of putting it."

"Which do you like better?"

He thought a minute. "I don't think I could choose. I like seeing ways to improve someone's living space. I like playing with designs. But the actual physical labor satisfies something in me as well. I suppose that's why I choose to do both.''

The old woman continued to stare at him while she digested his words.

Lizbeth folded the empty bags and turned from the cupboards. "There you are, Loretta. Everything put away neatly the way you like it."

"Thank you, Beth. You're a sweet child. Now…'' Her eyes sharpened. "…about that bill.''

Lizbeth dug into both pockets, then shrugged. "I guess it blew away.''

"That's what you said last week.''

"Did I?'' She was clearly blushing.

Watching it, Colin bit back a grin. It was obvious that lying didn't come easily to Lizbeth Sullivan. She was, in fact, just about the worst liar he'd ever met.

Lizbeth looked away. "I'm sorry, Loretta. I'll see that I take better care of your bill next week.''

"See that you do, child.'' The old woman shuffled toward the front door, with the cat following. When she pulled it open, she fixed Colin with a look. "Our Beth's one of the special ones, wouldn't you say?''

He nodded. "I would indeed. It was nice meeting you, Loretta. I hope I see you again.''

"Oh, I have a feeling you will, young man.''

She stood in the doorway and watched as he

helped Lizbeth into his truck. Then she reached
down and picked up her old cat.

"You liked him, didn't you, Brandi?"

The cat merely purred.

"So do I. But the question is, does our Beth like
him?" She scratched behind the cat's ears. "I
guess time will tell. But we'd better not let too
much time get past those two. Our Beth's already
wasted enough already."

Chapter 5

As soon as they stepped through the doorway of the cottage, Lizbeth glanced at the clock and gave a sound of dismay. "I'm afraid dinner is going to be a little late."

Before she could turn away Colin lay a hand on her arm, stopping her in mid-stride. "Hey. What's your hurry?"

She struggled to ignore the heat from his touch. "You've been working all day and..."

"So have you." He'd been ready for the little jolt when they touched. Still, it was unnerving. "Why don't you take the night off?"

"I don't under—"

"It's Friday night. Let's walk into town and eat at the Village Pub."

"Are you sure? The only thing they offer is beer and burgers."

"I'm up for that. How about you?"

She considered before nodding. "But it could be awfully crowded."

"I can handle a crowd. The question is can you?"

"I can if you can."

"Okay." He turned away. "I'll grab a shower and we'll go."

As he climbed the stairs he could still feel the tingling in his fingertips. How long, he wondered, could he pretend that there was nothing going on between them?

Every morning when he saw her looking so fresh and sweet and pretty he felt the jolt to his system. Every night when he lay in his bed, the thought of her lying just a room away taunted and teased him, making sleep difficult. Sooner or later he was going to have to deal with the feelings she aroused in him.

But not yet. Tonight they'd just relax and have some fun. With a woman like Lizbeth, he had the feeling he'd have to move very slowly. She was as skittish as a frightened colt.

He nudged his bedroom door shut and slipped out of his work clothes before stepping into the shower. A half hour later he was dressed and downstairs.

Lizbeth was in the parlor, entering figures in a ledger. She looked up when he paused in the doorway.

"That was fast." He was wearing dark pants and an oatmeal sweater, his dark hair still wet from the shower. And he was looking at her in that way that always did odd things to her heart.

"Come on." He held out his hand. "It's time you showed me the rest of your town."

She put away her ledgers, using the time to take a breath, hoping to calm her racing heart. Then she led the way out the front door and down the porch steps.

He paused. "Aren't you going to lock the door?"

She shook her head. "I haven't locked a door since I moved here. I doubt that anyone in Stafford would even consider such a thing."

He was grinning as he moved along beside her on the sidewalk. "I feel like I've just stepped back in time about a hundred years. Is this place for real?"

She joined in the laughter. "I thought the same thing at first. Now I'm so used to the idea, I never even question it. Everyone in Stafford looks out for everyone else."

He caught her hand and linked his fingers with hers. This time he was ready for the heat. "And you, most of all."

"Now why do you say that?" She looked down at their joined hands, before bringing her gaze to his.

"I see the way you take care of Loretta Mayfair. And I hear what people are saying. You're the one who supplies the food for the Yardley family's Fourth of July party, the church picnic, the town dance."

"I'm just being a good neighbor."

He paused, stared down into her eyes. "Yeah." He wondered if she knew how she looked. Despite the blush on her cheeks and the sweetness of that smile, she looked as tempting as sin. He touched a hand to her cheek. "Come on, neighbor. It's time I fed you."

The Village Pub was a gathering place for both young and old in Stafford. Along one wall was a bar that ran the length of the room. Every seat was taken. On the far side of the room were booths, occupied mainly by older, well-dressed couples. In the middle of the room were tables and chairs, some pulled together to accommodate entire families.

Everyone, it seemed, knew everyone. There were greetings exchanged, names shouted above the music that played in the background. Through this maze waitresses in black pants and white knit shirts carried trays that would stagger a weight lifter.

Colin spotted a table for two alongside the window and began leading Lizbeth toward it. As they snaked their way among tables, Lizbeth had to stop half a dozen times to exchange greetings. By the time they were seated she was flushed and a little breathless.

"Is there anyone here you don't know?"

She laughed and looked around. "I don't think so. They all look familiar. Except maybe that couple in the corner. I haven't seen them before. I'll bet they're the ones who bought the Granville place."

"Maybe you should go over and introduce yourself."

She looked at him more closely to see if he was teasing. Seeing the smile, she relaxed. "Maybe I will. After you feed me."

When the waitress came to their table she greeted Lizbeth warmly. Colin ordered two beers. Minutes later they sat sipping their drinks and studying the menu.

"What do you recommend?" he asked her. "The burger with mushrooms, or without?"

Lizbeth shrugged. "It's your call. Personally, I prefer the burger with everything. And the Pub's special fries."

"That good, huh?"

She nodded.

"Okay. We'll make it two."

He gave their order to the waitress and sat back to watch the passing crowd. Main Street was a parade of couples with strollers and wagons, their older children darting here and there as they chased each other in a game of tag. There were teens rollerblading. Older folks seated on benches, nodding greetings to their neighbors. Everyone in the town, it seemed, had spilled out of their homes to enjoy the warmth of a spring evening.

The ice cream parlor down the block was doing a brisk business. As was the deli across the street.

By the time the waitress brought them a second beer, a few of the tables had begun to empty. Older couples were eager to return to their homes and their favorite television shows or their bridge game with neighbors. Children fidgeted, eager to be outdoors before it grew too dark.

When the burgers and fries were served, the crowd had thinned. Most of those who remained were regulars. Young, hip businesspeople sprinkled with a few oldtimers who kept up a lively discussion of sports and politics.

After his first bite Colin looked over at Lizbeth. "You were right. This was worth waiting for."

"I thought you'd enjoy it. Sometimes, just thinking about the Pub's burgers has my mouth watering."

Colin found his mouth watering, too. But it wasn't for food. The sight of her, relaxed and happy, reminded him that all the burgers in the world wouldn't satisfy the appetite that was building inside him.

When the waitress returned to check on their drinks, Lizbeth shook her head. "I think I'd better have coffee now, Kim."

Colin nodded. "Make it two."

When they finished their meal and were sipping their coffee, he pointed to the row of video games along the wall. "Have you ever played?"

She shook her head.

"You're kidding. Never?"

"No. I don't even know what they are."

"I can see that your education in the finer things has been sorely lacking." He caught her hand. "Come on."

He led her to the bank of games and pulled her down on a seat beside him. "This is virtual auto racing. We'll be racing against each other."

"How?"

"You put your foot on the accelerator or brake, and keep your eye on that screen. The object is to beat my car to the finish line."

"That's all?"

"Uh-huh."

"Sounds easy enough."

He shot her a sideways glance as he dropped in some coins. Within seconds two cars appeared on the screen, their engines revving. A flag appeared, then suddenly lowered.

Her car remained at the starting line.

Colin nudged her elbow. "You have to hit the gas."

"Oh. Right." She floored the pedal and her car leapt ahead, then smashed into a brick wall.

She let out a shriek, followed by a giggle when she realized that everyone had turned to look at her.

Colin left his car idling, while he showed her how to slowly back up, then get her car onto the track. She floored the pedal again and sent her car careening over a low wall, a hydrant, a series of street signs and a flower bed, before smashing into a line of trees.

For a moment she looked horrified. Then, realizing it was only a game, and the cars on the screen would spring back to life with the touch of a pedal, she began laughing until tears streamed down her face. By the time she'd backtracked and returned to the race, the time was up.

"Oh, darn. I can't believe I wasted so much time." Her eyes were bright with pleasure. "It feels so real watching all that action on the screen. Especially when you're involved in a crash."

"Want to try again?"

"Yes. I know I can get the hang of this."

He dropped in more coins and watched as she

lowered the pedal slowly, keeping her car on a steady course along the track.

"Now you've got it," he called as his car passed hers.

"Maybe. But I'll never win like this." She floored the pedal and struggled to keep her car within the limits of her side of the track.

Their two cars raced head to head for several turns before Lizbeth took her eyes off the screen long enough to glance at Colin. The next thing she knew her car was swerving off the track and heading right for a high wall. She turned the wheel and overcorrected, sending the car into the grandstands, where people could be seen flying through the air while her car turned into a ball of fire.

Again she let out a shriek before bursting into gales of laughter.

"I'm hopeless at this."

"I wouldn't say hopeless. You managed to stay on track for a whole minute before killing half the fans who'd come to cheer you."

"That's just because I got careless. One more," she said. "And this time I intend to beat you."

"Really? Would you care to make a wager?"

"All right." Her eyes glittered with anticipation. "What should we play for?"

Oh, this was almost too easy. If he were a better man, he thought, he wouldn't take advantage of the situation. But what the hell. "How about a goodnight kiss?"

"You're on." She was smiling as he dropped in the coins. This time she was taking no chances. She eased down on the pedal and kept her gaze fixed on the screen, taking the first curve with ease, before moving into the second. She managed to avoid the various obstacles that were randomly tossed in her path. A dog, ambling across the track. A loose tire flying through the air, then landing directly in front of her car. When the path was clear she gathered speed as she took her car up the steep hill, and by the time she was headed down the other side she had the pedal floored.

She took the last curve of track almost a carlength ahead of Colin's vehicle, and was laughing hysterically as she headed for the finish line. "This time, Mr. St. James, I have you beat."

Just then, another racecar pulled out of the pits directly in front of her car. She twisted the wheel and her car turned sideways and slid across the inside of the track, smashing into one car after another before turning upside down and disintegrating.

She looked over to see Colin's car cross the finish line, to the cheers of the fans in the stands.

"Ah well." He turned toward her with a knowing smile. "Look at it this way. You get to walk home with a winner."

"I'll keep that in mind when I pay up."

He helped her to her feet and kept her hand in his. "This is one bet I can't wait to collect."

The streetlights had come on, casting soft yellow pools of light in the darkness. The moon was a slice of gold; the stars a scattering of diamonds. Walking along beside Colin, her hand still tucked in his, Lizbeth couldn't remember when she'd laughed this hard, or had such silly, spontaneous fun.

"I never would have found the nerve to try one of those games by myself."

"Really? Why?"

She shrugged. "For one thing, I had no idea they were such fun. I used to watch the people hooting and hollering while they played, and figured it took a lot of special skill to play." She laughed aloud. "I'm so glad we went to the Pub."

He looked over. "Even though I beat you?"

"Only because you've had more experience with that game. Give me another chance and I'll win."

"A glutton for punishment, I see."

"Oh, you're so smug. Now I'll have to risk it just to prove that I can win."

"Anytime, Ms. Sullivan. How about next Friday?"

"You're on."

"All right. It's a date."

A date. The very word had her stumbling, before she untangled her feet and managed to continue walking.

He paused beneath a streetlight and closed a hand over their linked hands. "You all right?"

"Yeah. Fine." But she had to look away quickly so he wouldn't see the sudden fear in her eyes. She'd just agreed to a real date. But then, wasn't that what this had been? And it had been fun. She hadn't felt clumsy or awkward. Of course, there hadn't been time to get all worked up about it. It had happened without rhyme or reason. Maybe that's why it had been so easy. But next Friday... She'd have a whole week to worry and fret and sweat about it.

They paused at the garden gate and Colin reached over to unlatch it before holding it open. When it swung closed they walked together to the porch and climbed the steps.

At the door he paused. "Want to sit awhile, or are you too tired?"

"I think I'll go up to bed now."

"All right. I think I'll stay out here." He touched a hand to his pocket. "Bill Yardley gave me one of his cigars today. This seems like a good time to smoke it."

"I'll say goodnight then." As she started to turn she felt his hand on her shoulder.

His voice, so close beside her, had her trembling. "Haven't you forgotten something?"

She'd forgotten nothing. But she'd hoped he had.

She turned. "Oh yes. The bet."

"That's right. There's the matter of that little debt you owe me, Lizbeth. And I intend to collect."

"All right." Determined to get it over with as quickly and painlessly as possible, she stood on tiptoe and brushed her lips over his.

He hadn't meant to kiss her back. In fact, all the way home he'd told himself to keep it light. He'd been certain he could carry it off. Until the moment her lips touched his. He'd allowed himself to sink into that cool, sweet innocence. And then, in the blink of an eye, everything changed.

His arms came around her, pinning her to the length of him. Those soft, tempting curves were pressed to his body, stirring his blood. She tasted so good he wanted to devour her, inch by tantalizing inch. And because she had gone so still and quiet, he took his time, sliding deeper into the kiss, pleasuring them both.

She was so warm. So sweet. So delicious. Steeped in pleasure, he moved his hands from her shoulders to her back to her waist. When he slid his hands under her sweater he found silk. And beneath that, warm, soft flesh. Flesh that seemed to melt at his touch.

She'd had no time to prepare herself. And now, with his mouth on hers, she couldn't breathe. With his hands skimming over her she couldn't move. Heart trembling, her legs threatening to fail her, she leaned weakly against the door, allowing him to kiss her, to touch her. A strange sound, like a soft animal purring, escaped her throat. She was helpless to stop it. Or to stop the heat that pulsed through her, sending the most amazing sparks through her already overcharged system.

He lingered over the kiss, unwilling to end it. Instead, he changed the angle and took it deeper. Took them both higher. And then, for good measure, higher still.

He felt the way she quivered in his arms. Heard the way her breath caught in her throat. And knew he'd taken her too far, too fast. But something perverse in his nature pushed him to take even more.

He nipped at her lower lip and absorbed the little shudders of breath that told him she was as close to the edge as he. One minute more, one tiny nudge, and they'd both tumble over the precipice and find themselves soaring.

As much as he wanted it, he knew she wasn't ready for this step.

Ever so slowly he eased back, keeping his hands steady at her shoulders.

Her skin was flushed. Her mouth still swollen from his kiss. Her breath was coming hard and fast. Her lids fluttered, then opened. She looked as stunned as he felt. But beneath that wide-eyed look of fear, he thought he detected something more. The unmistakable pull of desire.

That realization caused a little thrill of triumph.

He struggled to keep his tone light, despite the fact that he wanted, right this minute, to take her. Quick and fast. Here and now. And to hell with propriety. ''I can hardly wait to see what we'll play for next time.''

''I don't think…'' She swallowed, surprised at how difficult it was to speak over the dryness in her throat. ''I don't think we'd be wise to play for such stakes a second time.''

He skimmed a hand over her cheek and felt the heat. Stunned, he lowered it to his side, where he clenched it into a fist. ''Do we always have to be wise? Can't we just forget the rules sometimes, and do what makes us happy?''

''I've learned—'' her voice lowered with feeling ''—there's always a price to pay for breaking the rules.''

His eyes narrowed on hers. ''What price did you have to pay, Lizbeth?''

''I have to go in now. I'm feeling—'' she turned away and tore open the door, desperate to escape ''—really tired. Good night, Colin.''

He watched the flutter of her skirt as she hurried away. For long minutes he stood still, listening to the sound of her footsteps as she raced up the stairs. Then he turned and made his way to the glider, easing himself down, before pulling the cigar from his pocket. Light flared as he held a match to the tip. Then he leaned back.

He sat in the darkness, mulling over what she'd said. It was all beginning to make sense to him now.

Ever since he'd first seen her, he'd wondered why a beautiful, talented woman, so easy and open with everyone she knew, would seem to close up each time he got near.

She was like some wounded bird. In need of someone's tender ministrations, and yet afraid to allow anyone close enough to even touch her.

It was obvious that she'd been hurt. The question was, how deeply? Deep enough, it would seem, to keep her at arm's length from a man who'd been making no secret of his attraction to her.

So, did he want to pursue this further?

And if he did, would she ever allow him to get close enough to take this to another level? Or would she hide herself away, out of fear of being hurt even more?

"So, little bird." He exhaled a wreath of rich smoke. "What will it be? Do you hide away in your cage? Or do you risk it all and try to fly again?''

He leaned his head back to stare at the night sky. She might not be aware of it, but he'd detected a well of strength just beneath that shy sweet face she presented to the world.

He'd bet his money that, given the chance, she'd fly.

Chapter 6

Lizbeth was too agitated to undress. Besides, her hands were still trembling. She was afraid if she tried to unbutton her sweater, she'd tear off all the buttons. Instead she sank slowly to the edge of the bed and simply sat there.

She'd never, ever been kissed like that. Had never even known anyone could kiss like that. Her head was still spinning, her blood still too hot. And her heart. She touched a hand to the spot and felt the way it was thundering. Her poor heart might never be the same again.

What had just happened out there on the porch? How had a simple kiss turned into that… that…situation? She felt as she'd been thrust into some windowless airless room. She'd been afraid to breathe. Afraid to move, for fear of being devoured by some…monster.

Not a monster, she realized. She'd been afraid of being devoured by her own hunger.

She'd wanted him. Wanted to just tear off her clothes and give herself to him and beg him to end this need. Such a huge, hungry need to be held and loved by him.

Was it the same for Colin? Did he feel this over-powering need for her? Or was this just the way a man, any man, would act, as long as a woman permitted it? She didn't know. Oh, she wrapped her arms around herself and began to pace rest-lessly. That was the terrible part of all this. She simply didn't know.

She thought about her sisters. She could ask Alex, the family tomboy. She'd married Grant Ma-lone this past winter. Before the wedding, she'd confided that falling in love with Grant had been the most frightening, and the most wondrous, thing she'd ever experienced. But she hadn't seemed afraid. In fact, Lizbeth had never seen her older sister so blissfully happy.

They were so different, she and Alex. Alex had always been the fearless one. The one willing to set off on a trail, any trail, without a care in the world. Maybe she had once been that way, too, Lizbeth mused. But now that she was aware of the price exacted for hasty decisions, she'd become much more cautious. No, timid was the word that suited her now. She slapped a hand against the edge of the quilt. Timid. And she hated it.

She thought about phoning her younger sister, Celeste. Elegant, sophisticated Celeste would probably be able to recommend any number of high-minded texts on the subject of frigidity brought about by trauma and guilt. But then she would have to admit to Celeste that she'd spent these past ten years in nearly complete celibacy, except for a few disastrous attempts. And that she would never do. She simply couldn't imagine baring her soul's secrets to either of her sisters.

She would have to muddle through on her own.

Deep in thought, she went through the motions of removing her clothes and hanging them in the closet before slipping into a modest, white, eyelet trimmed nightgown.

Feeling as though she carried the weight of the world on her shoulders, she crawled into bed. But sleep wouldn't come. Instead she tossed and turned and thought about the way she'd felt in Colin's arms.

She hadn't believed she could ever feel like this. But what good would it do to encourage him? Sooner or later he'd find out that she was simply no good at sex.

There. She'd admitted it to herself.

A tear squeezed from the corner of her eye and she brushed it away with the heel of her hand. She wouldn't cry. She'd done enough of that to last a lifetime.

She rolled to her other side and punched her pillow, then scrunched her eyes tightly shut and began counting backwards from one thousand. It was a trick she'd taught herself years ago. And though it sometimes took her an hour or more, it kept her from allowing unpleasant thoughts to sneak in. She would not wallow in self-pity ever again.

Lizbeth lay in that pleasant limbo between being awake and asleep. She could feel the warmth of the morning sun as it slipped between a gap in the drapes and danced against her closed eyelids.

She was about to snuggle deeper under the blanket when she suddenly sat straight up in bed. Sunlight? What in the world was she doing drowsing away the morning. What time was it? A glance at the bedside clock told her she should have been downstairs fixing breakfast an hour ago.

She rushed through her shower and dressed hurriedly, leaving her damp hair to curl as it pleased. Then she raced downstairs and came to a skidding halt in the doorway of the kitchen.

"'Morning, sleepyhead.'' Colin was just pouring coffee into a mug. "Would you like some?''

"Thanks." It felt strange having someone else at home in her kitchen. "I'm sorry I'm late. I'll get breakfast started right away."

"No hurry." He handed her a cup and couldn't help smiling at the way she looked. As fresh as one of the flowers in her garden. And as sweet, in a long denim skirt and peppermint-striped shirt, her hair a riot of curls around a face that was, as usual, slightly flushed.

"Don't you have to get to the Yardley house?"

"Not today. It's Saturday."

"Oh." She hadn't remembered. In fact, her mind felt completely muddled. She blamed it on the fact that her sleep had been disrupted by so many dreams.

She resented the fact that Colin looked rested and refreshed. Apparently nothing had disturbed his sleep.

He drained his coffee. "I think I'll wash the truck."

"What about breakfast?"

"Don't bother. If I get hungry later I'll fix something. That is, if you don't mind having me in your kitchen."

"Don't think of it as mine. It's your kitchen too, for as long as you choose to stay at Stafford Cottage."

"Thanks. I'll remember that." He turned back to pour a second cup of coffee. Then he strolled out the door. Minutes later she heard the sound of running water. Through the window she watched as he used the hose to fill a bucket, and began to wash his truck.

With each movement his T-shirt strained against the ripple of muscles. He bent over the hood, scrubbing, polishing, and she studied those long muscular legs encased in tight-fitting jeans. He had the most beautifully sculpted body. She sipped her coffee and decided it wouldn't hurt to simply linger here a few minutes longer, indulging herself. After all, it was the weekend. And he was, quite simply, wonderful to watch.

Lizbeth couldn't believe the number of weeds that had found their way into her garden. Nestled between the peonies. Wrapped around the budding irises. They'd even taken root in the crevices between the rocks that formed a border along the side of the cottage wall.

She knelt in the grass and talked to the flowers as she filled the wheelbarrow.

"Just look at you. Aren't you pretty? That feeding of fertilizer I gave you last week must have done the trick. I don't think I've ever seen you looking so fine. In another week or two you're going to fill this little bed to overflowing with your blooms. Oh, sorry. I didn't mean to do that." She picked up a broken stem of flowers and nestled it in a basket. "But don't fret. You'll look just perfect on the dining room table tonight. Now, let's see if I can pull these weeds without disrupting any more of you…"

Out of the corner of her eye she caught sight of Colin leaning against the porch, his arms crossed over his chest, regarding her with a grin.

"You startled me. I didn't notice you there."

"Obviously. You were too busy talking to your buddies."

She flushed. "I suppose that's what comes of living alone. Pretty soon I'll be talking to the walls."

"Well, at least they won't talk back."

They both looked up as Jack Nowack unlatched the gate and walked up with a handful of mail.

"Afternoon, Jack."

He tipped his hat. "Beth. Colin." He turned to Lizbeth. "You got a letter from your grandfather."

"Oh, how nice." She slipped off her garden gloves and accepted the mail with a smile. "He'll be gearing up for another busy season."

"You think he'll ever retire?"

"Grandpa Sully?" She laughed and shook her head. "I can't imagine such a thing. He's like you, Jack. He just loves meeting people, stopping to chat with everyone who walks through the door of his inn in Lake Como. I can't imagine what he'd do if he didn't have that to look forward to."

"Well." The older man paused to polish his sunglasses. "Seems to me his granddaughter takes after him." He slipped the glasses on and turned to Colin. "Bill and Sue Yardley gave me a tour of their place. You're doing some fine work."

"Thanks." It occurred to Colin that there were no secrets in Stafford.

Jack smiled at Lizbeth. "My wife wanted me to thank you for the cupcakes you baked for our daughter's birthday. She said little Taylor was the most popular girl in school."

"I'm glad she and her classmates enjoyed them."

Lizbeth waited until he walked away and latched the gate. Then she dropped down in the grass and tore open her grandfather's letter.

"Are you finished weeding?"

She looked up, surprised to see Colin standing beside the wheelbarrow. "Yes. I'll empty that in a little while."

"I'll do it. You read your letter."

He picked up her gardening tools and shoved the wheelbarrow toward the potting shed, leaving her alone to savor the news from her grandfather.

Minutes later Lizbeth tucked the letter into her pocket and looked around at the sound of hammering.

She walked toward the shed, where Colin was repairing some loose hinges.

He looked over his shoulder as she approached. "If these had pulled free, you were in danger of losing this door."

"I know. I kept meaning to fix them. But there always seemed to be something more important that needed my attention."

"Like that?" He pointed toward the rear fence, lined with budding lilac and magnolia trees.

Lizbeth shook her head in defeat. "I know those broken pickets need replacing. But they're just one more thing that will have to wait until I have the time and money."

"No time like now." He tested the door. Satisfied that the hinges were solid, he strode toward the back fence, with Lizbeth trailing behind.

"This isn't such a big job." He began pulling away the rotted boards.

"It isn't? Byron Porterfield told me it would take him a couple of days and cost me at least three hundred dollars in supplies and labor."

"That's if he had to buy the wood cut to size from a lumber company, then install it and paint it. But what if I buy a couple of boards and cut them myself? Would you mind painting them?"

"Of course not."

"Good. I think if we work together we could have the fence repaired by this evening. And all for the cost of a couple of pieces of lumber and a little paint."

"Oh, Colin. Could we?"

"I don't mind if you don't." He glanced at her in that way that always had the breath catching in her throat. "But while I'm picking up the lumber and paint, you might want to change. You do own something besides all those fancy lady clothes, don't you?"

She glanced down at herself, then laughed delightedly. "Of course I do."

She turned away, the hem of her skirt dancing around her ankles.

As he strolled to his truck it occurred to Colin that he'd be very happy if she decided to put on a pair of skimpy shorts. But that was probably too much to ask of the very prim and proper Lizbeth Sullivan.

They weren't shorts. But she wore a pair of faded jeans that hugged her bottom. And what a shapely one it was, Colin thought as he bent to his table saw. She'd topped them with a cast-off shirt worn loose. But after a few minutes she realized the shirttails were brushing across the fresh paint, and she'd had no choice but to tie them midriff-style to keep them out of the way.

Much better, Colin thought with an appreciative smile. There was just a hint of pale white flesh teasing him as she moved the paint brush back and forth in smooth, even strokes.

The freshly-cut pickets lay across a pair of saw horses. As soon as Lizbeth had finished painting them on one side she turned them over and neatly painted them on the other. Though the work was tedious, she attacked it with a vengeance.

Colin took a break from his sawing. "I can see you've painted a time or two."

She nodded. "Every wall in the cottage."

"You did it yourself?"

"Of course." She looked up. "I also hung the wallpaper, sewed the drapes and upholstered several of the chairs in the parlor."

"Uh-huh. And you also bring home the bacon, fry it up in the pan. 'Cause you are woman," he sang off-key.

She couldn't help laughing at his teasing. "That's right. And don't you forget it."

He gave her a long, slow look that had her cheeks turning pink. "Believe me, lady, I'm not apt to forget that."

She returned to her painting, acutely aware of the appreciative glances he kept sending her way.

A short time later he finished cutting the last board. By then, the first pickets were dry, and he was able to begin nailing them to the fence rails. Before long, with the sun directly overhead, he'd tossed aside his shirt and bent to his work in earnest.

Lizbeth found herself so distracted by the sight

of him that she could hardly concentrate on her job. She stared, fascinated at the play of muscles along his shoulders and back. With each ring of the hammer against a nail she felt a similar ping to her heart.

He cocked his head and caught her staring. "You almost done there?"

"Hmm? Oh, yes." She took a final swipe of paintbrush over wood, then set the brush aside.

"Maybe you could start handing the dry ones to me."

"Sure." She picked up a length of picket and carried it to him.

"Thanks." He smiled, and it occurred to her that he had the most wonderful smile in the world. "If you could just hold it in place here, I'll drive in the first nail. Then while I'm finishing, you can get the next piece. We'll have this job done in no time."

Without even being conscious of it, they developed a rhythm. Lizbeth choosing a length of wood, fitting it in place and holding it until the first nail had been driven to hold it securely. Colin finishing the job, while she moved on to the next, and the next.

Less than an hour later Colin nailed the last board in place. Then they stood back to admire their handiwork.

"Oh, Colin. It's beautiful."

"Yeah." His body slick with sweat, he picked up his wadded T-shirt and used it to towel his face before he shot her a grin that had her heart doing a series of somersaults. "We make a good team, don't you think?"

She nodded.

He turned away to dismantle the table saw and coil the extension cord, before heading for his truck. For a minute longer Lizbeth watched him. Then she picked up the bucket of paint and the brushes.

With a rag and water from the hose she began to clean the brushes, before wiping the paint from her hands.

"Just what I needed." Colin walked over and picked up the hose, before helping himself to a long drink.

He held the spray toward her. "Want one?"

"Yes. I'm parched." She leaned close and allowed the icy spray to flow into her mouth.

"Umm. That's wonderful." Smiling, she used the rag to dry her chin.

"Wait a minute. You missed a spot." He tossed the hose aside and reached for the rag in her hands. Before she could ask what he meant he cupped her chin in his hand and dabbed the rag to a spot of paint on her cheek.

Maybe it was the heat of the day, or the satisfaction of a job well done. Certainly the mood was enhanced by the proximity of his naked, sweating chest, and the fact that they'd worked so closely together all afternoon. Still, they both seemed caught off guard by the sudden storm that engulfed them at that single touch.

One minute they were laughing together. The next, his big hands were framing her face. His eyes, so blue they seemed to burn with an inner fire, were fixed on hers.

Her hands reached up and closed over his wrists, before sliding up his arms. Her smile faded as, without even realizing what she was doing, she stood on tiptoe to reach his mouth.

He'd had no time to prepare. All he knew was that her mouth was on his. Willingly. Without any effort on his part. And now the explosion of feeling was ripping through him. Tearing him apart, piece by piece, until he jerked back, feeling as if he'd just taken a grenade to the chest.

He saw her eyes go wide. Knew that his reaction had stunned her. And then, because she looked as if she might turn and run, he dragged her close and held on. His hands massaged her upper arms, her shoulders, then his fingers began tangling in all those silken curls. On a moan of desperation, he lowered his face to hers and captured her mouth, hungry for another taste.

She was so sweet. And so afraid. He could taste her fear. He wanted, more than anything, to soothe it. To stop the trembling he could feel on her lips as he traced them with his tongue before taking more.

He could feel his blood heating, surging in his veins. Could hear it roaring like thunder in his temples. Could feel a mist of passion clouding his vision. And he was helpless to stop it. She was so sweet, so good, so innocent. She was, quite simply, everything he'd ever wanted. The woman of his dreams.

It took him a moment to realize that she'd gone very still in his arms.

He drew in a breath and took a step back. But it wasn't far enough, or fast enough for Lizbeth. She could still feel the heat from his body. Could still feel the shocking vibrations she'd absorbed at the first contact with his naked chest. Could still taste the passion.

Colin had learned his lesson the previous night. This time there would be no recriminations. No serious discussion. The best way to handle this was to keep it light.

He forced a smile. "Well, as I see it, we have two choices here."

"Choices?" She struggled to focus.

"Yeah." His smile grew. "I can go grab a cold shower before dinner. Or, if you've a mind to, you could join me and…scrub my back, or something."

She was determined to follow his lead this time. If he could smile after what they'd just shared, so could she. "It's the 'or something' that might be a problem. Why don't you shower alone and I'll do the same."

"Spoilsport."

She managed to turn off the hose, aware that her hand only shook a little. Over her shoulder she called, "But since I helped you with the fence, I don't see why you can't help me with dinner."

"I'll do even better." He nodded toward the charcoal grill stored alongside the potting shed. "Before I shower I'll get a fire started in the grill. And after I've cleaned up, I'll make dinner."

When she opened her mouth to protest, he lifted a hand. "In fact, I'll even provide dessert. Now why don't you go take a long, leisurely bath or something."

She couldn't help laughing. He was a constant surprise. "There's that 'or something' again."

"Yeah." He shot her a wicked grin. "So if you're smart, you'll get out of here before I decide just what that might be."

Chapter 7

Lizbeth hurried to her room, wondering at the feelings swirling inside her. Why should she feel so excited at the prospect of Colin fixing dinner? After all, it was only a simple barbeque. But it had been so long since anyone had cooked for her. She supposed it was because she was so competent in the kitchen. Most of her friends here in Stafford were more than happy to let her do something she took such pride in. But here she was, about to let someone else cook for her. Feed her. And the anticipation was delightful.

She stripped off her paint-stained clothes and settled into warm, fragrant bathwater. It felt so good to soak after a day of hard, challenging work.

After scrubbing the last of the paint smears, she stepped from the tub, her skin glowing, her wet hair wrapped in a towel.

She blew her hair dry and left it to fall in soft, loose curls secured off her face with combs. Then she slipped into a knit dress of pale peach with a softly rounded neckline and a long column of skirt that fell to her ankles. On her feet were canvas slippers in the same shade of peach.

When she descended the stairs she caught the wonderful scent of meat and vegetables cooking on the grill. She couldn't wait to see what Colin had prepared. Her step was light as she raced toward the dining room and glanced at the small round table beside the bay window. Except for the bouquet of peonies she'd set earlier in the center of the table, it was empty.

With a shrug, she made her way to the kitchen. But that table was empty as well.

Puzzled, she crossed the kitchen and threw open the back door.

Colin was standing beside the grill, turning something that smelled simply wonderful. Beyond him, in the middle of a grassy area, was a blanket, set with plates and silverware. A bottle of wine protruded from a small ice bucket.

"Colin. A picnic." She flew down the steps toward him. "Oh, how lovely."

He had to absorb a jolt at the sight of her. With

all that porcelain skin and that tangle of golden curls, and that regal-looking dress swirling around her ankles, she reminded him of a beautiful, fragile princess from some other time and place.

"It was too perfect to spend indoors. Who knows when we'll get another day like this? Do you mind?"

"Mind?" She clasped her hands together. "It's a wonderful idea." She peered over his shoulder. "What're you fixing?"

"Shish kabob. A little beef, a little chicken and whatever vegetables I could find in the refrigerator, basted with my own special, secret ingredients."

"Special secret ingredients?" She breathed in. "It smells wonderful."

"So do you." He leaned closer and inhaled the fragrance of spring flowers that always seemed to surround her.

She took a step back. He was simply too potent. Too...male. "Would you like some wine?"

"Yeah. And I'll turn these one more time until they're done."

He watched as she walked to the blanket and knelt beside the ice bucket, filling two glasses. Every movement was sheer poetry. There was just something about a woman in all those clothes that made him itch to get her out of them.

When she walked back and handed him a glass, he kept his eyes steady on hers while he lifted it to his lips and tasted. His smile was quick and dangerous. "Now that's just what I needed. Thanks." He nodded toward the blanket in the grass. "I hope you don't mind that I borrowed that from the foot of my bed."

She laughed. "I don't think you'll be needing it anytime soon. Unless we get a cold snap."

"Yeah. That's what I figured. I'll make sure I shake the grass out of it before I take it back indoors."

"I should hope so. Or some poor unsuspecting guest months from now might unfold it in the middle of the night and wake up with bits of grass stuck to his skin."

"We wouldn't want to give Stafford Cottage a bad reputation." He was still staring at her in that direct manner.

She could feel her cheeks growing warm. But she couldn't seem to look away. "Not when I've worked so hard to make it perfect."

"Like you." He saw the way her face flamed. He touched a hand to her arm. "Sorry. I just meant that you seem almost too good to be true."

"No one is that good."

"You are." He kept his hand on her arm, even though he knew it made her uncomfortable. "Do you work at it? Or does it just come naturally?"

"You don't know me, Colin. You don't know anything about me."

"I know that you're unerringly kind and generous with your neighbors. You're thoughtful. You look out for an elderly woman without ever letting her know what you're doing. You conveniently lose a receipt rather than let her see what you spent out of your own pocket. And then you give yourself away when you try to lie, because you're so bad at it."

"But I…"

He touched a finger to her mouth to stop her protest. "You're so tender-hearted you can't even bear to break off a flower stem without apologizing. And on top of all that, you're so easy to look at, I sometimes find myself staring at you just for the pure pleasure of it."

"Well…" Because she had no idea how to react to all this flattery, she simply sipped her wine. "I guess I won't disillusion you by telling you about all my flaws."

She shifted her gaze to the grill. "Do you think our dinner is ready yet?"

"Yeah." He couldn't help smiling at her discomfort. It was just so appealing.

He handed her his glass. "Why don't you top off our drinks, and I'll get this food on a plate."

She turned away, grateful for something to do.

Minutes later he sat beside her on the blanket and began to serve her plate. There were skewers of meat and vegetables, as well as a foil packet of seasoned rice that sent up a fragrant cloud when he cut it open.

"Hungry?" he asked.

"Starving."

His deep blue gaze met hers. Held. "Yeah. Me, too."

And, he thought, if he didn't soon feed the hunger that simmered inside, there was no telling what he might do. Hunger, especially the kind that tormented him, could drive a man to the edge. And beyond.

She tasted, then turned to him with a look of surprise. "This is really wonderful. I hope you'll let me on the secret of your marinade."

"Hmm. Careful." He regarded her over his wine. "It might cost you."

She laughed. "Is nothing free with you?"

"Not free exactly. But I could make the payments extremely painless."

"Another kiss, I suppose."

He arched one villainous brow. "That's a given. But there'd be more."

"Like what?" She nibbled her dinner, and found that she was beginning to enjoy his teasing banter. He had such a delightful sense of humor it was impossible not to get caught up in his silliness.

"Well, there's your legs, for instance."

"My legs?" She lowered her fork.

"Yeah. Are you sure you have some?"

"Now what is that supposed to mean?"

He wiggled his brows. "All I ever get to see is skirt and more skirt. You wear yours so long, I'm not sure there are any legs under there. Don't you own a pair of shorts?"

"Well." She picked up her wine, getting into the spirit. "I've been told, by men who've seen them, of course, that I have fabulous legs. Actually they're movie-star-quality legs. But that's why I feel compelled to keep them covered. Men have been known to kill for a glimpse of legs like mine. I simply couldn't have such a thing on my conscience."

He threw back his head and roared, before touching a hand to his head and giving a mock groan of pain. "No more. I can't stand to hear any more. Especially when I'm not allowed to see these fabulous movie-star legs."

"Life is hard." She sipped her wine. "We all have our little burdens."

"Yeah. Well, here's another one. If I ever give you my recipe, the price will be a glimpse of those movie-star legs."

He was still laughing as he finished his dinner. She constantly surprised him. And delighted him.

Still…he'd give a lot to see those carefully hidden legs of hers.

"Colin, that was really good." Lizbeth helped him clear away the dishes and set them on a tray before glancing around. "But didn't you promise me dessert?"

"I was pretty sure you wouldn't forget about that." He shook the blanket, then folded it over his arm before taking the tray from her hands. "I'll be back in a minute."

True to his word, he was gone only a minute before returning to the backyard. Seeing that his hands were empty she gave him an arched look.

"Okay. Where's dessert?"

"We have to take a walk for it."

"A walk?"

He nodded. "To the ice cream parlor."

"Oh. It's the perfect night for it. What a great idea." She danced along beside him and paused as he opened the garden gate. Then they started up the sidewalk that led into town.

As they walked Lizbeth waved to a boy on a bicycle who shot past them before saying, "That's Billy Barton, who delivers the paper."

She waved to a couple cruising past in their car. "Reverend Watson and his wife, Mary Lyn."

"And this guy?" Colin nodded toward a man in sweats huffing toward them. "He looks familiar."

"You met him at the drugstore. That's Seth Simpson, getting his evening workout." She smiled. "Evening, Seth."

"Beth. Colin. A grand night for a walk." He strode briskly past, without waiting for their reply.

When they reached Main Street they realized they weren't the only ones with ice cream on their minds. They stood in line with a dozen others, waiting their turn.

"What's your pleasure?" Colin asked when they found themselves at the front of the line.

"I think I'll try a strawberry sundae."

"Okay. Then I'll get a hot fudge." He winked. "That way I'll get to taste two different flavors."

She gave him an imperious look. "You will, providing I'm willing to share."

"I'll give you a taste of my hot fudge."

She rolled her eyes. "You know just what buttons to push, don't you, Colin St. James?"

He leaned close to whisper in her ear, "If that were true, Ms. Sullivan, I'd already have you in my bed." He saw the quick flush on her cheeks and added, "But here I am, muddling through as best I can, with absolutely no help from you at all."

She didn't know what caught her more by surprise. His admission that he wanted her, or her pleasure at hearing it put into words. There was no denying the thrill that shot straight through her.

Feeling more daring than ever, she gave him a smile filled with devilment. "Oh. It's my help you want, is it? And all this time I thought the only thing you wanted from me was my good cooking.''

"Believe me, Ms. Sullivan. A man would be willing to starve, as long as he knew he could…indulge his other hunger.''

"Speaking of hunger…'' Lizbeth nodded toward the teenage girl behind the counter who took his money and handed him a tray.

They carried their ice cream sundaes to a circular table on a small patio outdoors. When they were seated, Colin handed Lizbeth her sundae, then watched as she took the first taste.

With a smile she dipped her spoon into it a second time and held it to his mouth.

"You're really going to share?''

"It's only fair.'' She grinned. "Since you'll then have to share that hot fudge with me. And in case I didn't mention it earlier, next to strawberry, hot fudge is my favorite.''

"Okay. Fair's fair.'' He dipped his spoon in his own sundae and offered her a taste.

Seeing a drop of fudge on her lower lip he leaned closer and touched a finger to the spot. "I was going to kiss it off, but I figured, with all your friends and neighbors watching, you'd have a lot of explaining to do.''

She chuckled. "Would I ever.''

He paused. "Would that bother you?''

She was still laughing. "I don't know. It's never happened to me before."

"Well then." Without warning he leaned closer and brushed his mouth over hers. "Let's find out just how you feel about it," he whispered against her lips.

She felt the jolt to her system and thought about pulling back, but it was impossible to move. And then, when he moved his tongue over her lower lip, she absorbed a series of tremors that had her hands fisting in her lap.

He drew back slowly, watching her eyes. They were so expressive, revealing every single emotion she was experiencing.

"Well." He picked up his spoon. "Except for a few glances our way, no one seemed to mind that I kissed you. How do you feel about being kissed in public?"

She strove to keep it light. "I'd say, after strawberry and hot fudge sundaes, it might become my next favorite thing."

"Yeah?" He gave her a wicked smile and turned toward her. "Maybe we should do it again."

She put a hand on his chest. "Not a chance. One public kiss is all you get. Besides, you're melting my ice cream."

With the sound of their neighbors' voices carried on the warm evening breeze, they took their time, enjoying the food and the company and the fading light of evening.

Later, with the moon high and the sky a glittering canopy of light, they walked home. It seemed the most natural thing in the world to link fingers as they walked.

When they reached the cottage, Colin unlatched the gate and held it open while Lizbeth started up the walk. He caught up with her at the bottom of the porch.

"Sit with me awhile."

"All right." She sat on the glider and he settled himself beside her, his arm around her shoulders.

They listened to the sounds of the night. The hum of insects. The occasional call of a night bird. A boy whistling for his dog.

Colin stretched out his long legs. "I can't remember when I've had such a simple, satisfying day. From beginning to end it's been like some kind of wonderful gift."

"It was the same for me, Colin." She felt a curl of pleasure as his fingers played with the ends of her hair. This time she didn't question if he knew what his touch did to her. He knew exactly what he was doing. And so did she. "I wish it didn't have to end."

"It doesn't, Lizbeth."

His voice sounded a little too deep. A little too rough. She turned her head to study him. In the moonlight his eyes were the color of midnight. In profile his rugged, craggy features made her think of a man accustomed to taking what he wanted.

She lay a hand over his. "All good things come to an end."

"Is that what you believe?" He turned her hand over, running his thumb over her palm, all the while staring deeply into her eyes. "Has everything good in your life always come to an end, Lizbeth?"

She felt a stab, sharp and quick, around her heart and lowered her head. "Yes."

He caught her chin and forced her to look at him. "It doesn't have to be that way."

"Doesn't it?" She knew her lips were quivering and she hated that even now, after all these years, she could be moved by her memories. "If there's one thing I've learned, it's that nothing good lasts forever."

"If you believe that, then why not reach for whatever happiness you can today, and to hell with tomorrow?" He touched a hand to her cheek and leaned close until his breath whispered over her face. "You have to know that I want you, Lizbeth. Desperately."

"I know. And I want…" She couldn't say the words. It simply wasn't possible for her to put such intimate thought into words. "But I need…time."

He touched his forehead to hers and expelled a long, slow breath. "Take all the time you want."

She swallowed. "I think I'll go up to bed now."

"All right."

He started to draw back, but she touched a tentative finger to his cheek. "I wouldn't mind, though, if you kissed me goodnight."

He closed his eyes a moment, gathering patience. "I'm not sure that's a good idea."

He could see the way she withdrew into herself and mentally cursed. She was so timid. So insecure. As she started to get up he stood beside her and offered his hand. He walked her to the door, then brushed his lips lightly over hers. Even that tiny butterfly kiss was enough to rock him back on his heels.

"Good night, Lizbeth. Sweet dreams."

"Good night, Colin." She let herself into the house and quickly climbed the stairs.

He remained where he was. Watching and listening as the night closed in around him. And wondering how much longer he could hold all this passion in check before he simply exploded.

Chapter 8

Lizbeth stood in the afternoon sunshine, gathering the sheets off the line and folding them into a big wicker basket. The week had gone by in a blur of work. Shopping, cooking, running errands, as well as baking all sorts of special treats for the annual town dance, the Spring Fling.

She'd thought all the hard work would help keep her mind off Colin. But the simple truth was, nothing could distract her for long. Every time she saw him fresh from the shower, or coming in after a day of work at the Yardley home, she felt familiar twinges of need and guilt.

She paused in her work. What was she going to do about him? Some nights, when she crawled into bed, she taunted herself with thoughts of going to him and simply throwing herself into his arms. But a good stern talking-to usually managed to dissuade her from such foolishness. Still, there had been a few nights when she'd missed a great deal of sleep because of him. The temptation seemed to be getting stronger with every passing day.

She chided herself for wasting time daydreaming when she should be using this time to think about what she would fix for dinner. She'd been planning a ginger-mustard chicken with a Thai cucumber salad, and for dessert, apple crisp. Was that robust enough for a man like Colin who put in such long hours on the job?

She was still mulling the menu as she lifted the basket.

Suddenly she heard Loretta's voice coming from the other side of the fence. "Oh, I remember when I used to hang my laundry. I can still smell how fresh everything was when I'd bring it indoors."

"I know. It just seems to bring the springtime right into the house." Lizbeth lowered the basket to the ground and walked closer. "Enjoying the sunshine?"

The older woman nodded. "Brandi and I needed some fresh air."

They both smiled at the antics of the old cat, crouching in the grass, waiting to attack a dandelion waving in the breeze.

When Colin's truck pulled into the drive and came to a smooth stop, both women turned to watch as he climbed down and made his way toward them.

From her vantage point on the other side of the fence Loretta watched the way Lizbeth's eyes softened at the sight of him. "Have you asked your young man to the Spring Fling?"

Instantly Lizbeth's chin came up. "He isn't my young man, Loretta. And I haven't asked him."

"For heaven's sake, why not?" The old woman chanced a quick glance at her young neighbor's slightly flushed face. "Are you afraid he might say yes?"

That hit a nerve. Lizbeth was grateful that, before she could think of a reply, Colin called out a greeting.

"Hello, ladies."

When he paused beside the fence Loretta said, "You're just the man I wanted to see, Colin St. James."

"Really?" He gave her a friendly smile. "What about?"

"It's about our town dance, the Spring Fling, being held tomorrow night." She ignored Lizbeth's look of stunned surprise. "I was wondering if you had a date for it."

He couldn't bite back the smile that caught at

the corner of his lips. "As a matter of fact I don't. Would you like to be my date?"

Her smile was positively beaming. "I certainly would. I thought you'd never ask. But it's too far to walk to town. I believe I'll need to ride in that vehicle." She pointed to his truck.

"It would be my pleasure, Loretta. What time would you like me to come by for you?"

"Oh, half past seven would be just fine." She turned to Lizbeth. "If you won't worry that you're horning in on my date, you're welcome to ride along, Beth."

"Gee, thanks, Loretta." Lizbeth's frown grew in direct proportion to Colin's grin. "That's very kind of you."

The old woman held up a hand. "Not at all. I hope you don't mind, Colin? I know three's a crowd. But it seems silly for Beth to walk when we'll be going in her direction anyway."

"I'd be happy to bring Lizbeth along. Maybe, if you wouldn't object, I could dance with her once or twice."

"Now, now." Loretta was clearly enjoying herself. "Our Beth has work to do. She hosts the dessert table, you know. Very important job. She hardly ever dances with anyone at our annual dance. Oh, except Reverend Watson." The old woman's eyes were twinkling with mischief. "I suppose he's safe enough." She turned away, lean-

ing heavily on her cane. "Well, I'll see you tomorrow night, Colin." Then she seemed to think
of something more and turned back. "In case
you're thinking of bringing me a corsage, I'll be
wearing a rose satin dress."

Colin winked. "I'll remember."

She glanced at her young neighbor. "What color
dress will you be wearing, Beth?"

"Um. White, I think."

"White?" The old woman frowned. "Don't you
have something a bit more daring? Like red? Or
hot pink?"

"Hot pink?" Lizbeth shot her an incredulous
look. "Loretta, what's come over you?"

The old woman shrugged, then glanced at Colin
and smiled. "I guess it's true what they say. It's a
pity that youth is wasted on the young." She
waved a hand. "I'll see you tomorrow night, Colin.
I can't wait to see how you'll look in a suit and
tie. Oh, and I'll see you tomorrow night, too,
Beth."

Colin turned away and busied himself lifting the
basket of laundry to hide the laughter that was
nearly choking him. Loretta Mayfair might be
ninety-two. But in her heart she was about nine-
teen, and full of the devil.

Lizbeth stood in front of the full-length mirror
in her room and studied her reflection. Loretta was

right, she thought with a sigh of disgust. The white dress she'd planned to wear to the dance was bland. Like her. Bland and so sticky-sweet she wanted to gag. High-necked, long-sleeved, and completely uninspiring. She unzipped the back of the dress and tossed it on her bed, then began rummaging through her closet for something else. She tried on a yellow dress that made her look like a daisy. A pink chiffon that she'd worn in a friend's wedding. All she needed was a basket of flowers to look like the proverbial bridesmaid.

A glance at the clock had her tearing frantically through her closet. She could already hear the shower running in the other room and knew that Colin would be dressed and downstairs waiting for her.

Oh, what to wear?

She studied the designer dress her sister Celeste had sent her from New York. She'd never worn it, simply because she thought it completely unsuitable for the town of Stafford. It was, to her way of thinking, a big-city dress. Sleek. Sophisticated. And not at all what she would have ever chosen for herself. Furthermore, the narrow straps at the shoulders and the low, low back made it impossible to wear anything under it.

She fingered the column of Chinese red silk and decided to slip it on just to satisfy her curiosity.

Once she had, she would simply discard it with the others that littered her bed.

As soon as the silk whispered over her flesh and settled at her ankles, she studied herself in the mirror with a look of astonishment. Oh, it was anything but bland. It was hot. It was sexy. It was…simply wonderful. And unlike anything she'd ever worn before.

Caught up in the moment, she brushed her hair long and loose, then pulled it behind one ear with a jeweled comb. Then she dug out a pair of black strappy sandals she hadn't worn in more than a year, and a tiny black beaded bag. She added gloss to her lips, then studied herself critically.

She looked positively sinful. She couldn't wait to see Loretta's eyes.

Not to mention Colin's.

Pressing a hand to the butterflies in her stomach, she tore open her door and headed down the stairs before she could lose her nerve and talk herself out of it.

Even before she reached the bottom step she saw Colin standing in the hallway. At her footfall he turned, his hands behind his back. Though he said not a word, the look on his face spoke volumes.

His gaze moved slowly over her from the top of her head to the tips of her toes peeking from the sandals. He cleared his throat. ''Excuse me for

NO POSTAGE
NECESSARY
IF MAILED
IN THE
UNITED STATES

BUSINESS REPLY MAIL
FIRST-CLASS MAIL   PERMIT NO. 717   BUFFALO, NY

POSTAGE WILL BE PAID BY ADDRESSEE

SILHOUETTE READER SERVICE
3010 WALDEN AVE
PO BOX 1867
BUFFALO NY 14240-9952

If offer card is missing write to: Silhouette Reader Service, 3010 Walden Ave., P.O. Box 1867, Buffalo NY 14240-1867

GET FREE BOOKS
and a
FREE GIFT WHEN YOU PLAY THE...

LAS VEGAS
GAME

*Just scratch off the gold box
with a coin. Then check
below to see the gifts you get!*

YES!
I have scratched off the gold Box. Please send me my
2 FREE BOOKS and **gift for which I qualify.** I understand
that I am under no obligation to purchase any books
as explained on the back of this card.

▼ DETACH AND MAIL CARD TODAY! ▼

345 SDL C6RA

245 SDL C6Q5
(S-IM-OS-02/01)

NAME (PLEASE PRINT CLEARLY)

ADDRESS

APT.#   CITY

STATE/PROV.   ZIP/POSTAL CODE

7	7	7	Worth TWO FREE BOOKS plus a BONUS Mystery Gift!
🍒	🍒	🍒	Worth TWO FREE BOOKS!
🔔	🔔	♣	TRY AGAIN!

staring, miss. I was waiting for Lizbeth Sullivan. Have you seen her?''

She laughed and shook her head, sending golden curls dancing. ''She decided she couldn't make it tonight. She's sending me along as her substitute.''

''Then I suppose I'd better give these to you.'' In his hand was a nosegay of perfect red roses, tied with lace.

''Oh, Colin.'' Moved to tears she lifted the flowers to her face and breathed in their perfume, struggling for composure. ''How did you know what color to get?''

''You said you'd be wearing white. I thought these would add some color. But I'm afraid they're extremely dull next to you, Lizbeth.''

She glanced down at herself, still amazed at her boldness. ''You don't think it's too…daring?''

He shook his head, unable to tear his gaze from her. ''You look so beautiful I'm speechless. Come on. Let's see what Loretta has to say about this.''

He offered his hand and she accepted, taking the last two steps without even feeling them beneath her feet.

He kept her hand tucked in his as he led her outside and helped her into the truck. They drove the short distance to her neighbor's house in silence. When he came to a stop at Loretta's door he turned with a smile. ''Okay. Come with me while I pick up my date.''

They were both laughing as they walked up the path. Even before Colin had a chance to knock, the door was pulled open and Loretta stood framed in the doorway. When she caught sight of Lizbeth her smile grew until she was positively beaming. "Now that's what I call a dress fit for dancing. Don't you agree, Colin?"

"I certainly do. And I must say, Loretta, you look ready for a dance or two as well."

She ran a hand down the skirt of her lovely rose-colored dress, fresh from the cleaners. "Thank you. I do favor strong colors. And even stronger perfume."

"Then these should do nicely." He held out his hand to reveal a corsage of glossy white gardenias. "I bought these for my date."

"Oh, Colin." She breathed in the fragrance and sighed. "My Henry bought me gardenias on our first date. And every year on our anniversary he bought them for me, knowing how much I loved them. How could you possibly know?"

He shrugged. "Call it an educated guess. Helped along by the woman at the florist shop, who mentioned that you had a fondness for them."

"Oh, you." Her eyes misty, Loretta touched a hand to his cheek.

He reached for her shawl. "Would you like me to carry that?"

She handed it over, then reached down and petted her cat. "Don't wait up, Brandi," she cooed. "I think I'm going to be out very late tonight with the best looking man in Stafford."

With a laugh, Colin offered an arm to each of the women and led them toward his truck.

"This is a bit of a climb, " Lizbeth called as she settled herself in the middle.

Colin easily lifted Loretta up to the seat and handed up her shawl and cane before walking around to the driver's side. Lizbeth felt a little shiver when his thigh pressed against hers. He glanced over and smiled as he turned the key in the ignition. From her position Loretta watched. And in the darkness gave a nod of smug satisfaction.

The annual Spring Fling was held in the community center, a converted mansion in the heart of town, which housed the arts council, the historical society and the garden club. Each organization had been busy for weeks turning the old building and its grounds into a showplace. And because each club tried to outdo the other, it was a dazzling display.

The lighted walkway was lined with showy tulips and daffodils, and beds of fragrant peonies. Twinkling lights had been strung in the huge old lilac bushes and magnolia trees that were heavy with blossoms. Inside, the air was perfumed with lavish bouquets of spring flowers.

The huge, domed entrance foyer had been turned into a gallery displaying local artists' wares. The walls were hung with framed watercolors and portraits. Several pieces of pottery and even some oversized bronzes were positioned around the room. The effect was at once elegant and charming.

The meeting room had been transformed into a grand ballroom. Ancient chandeliers had been polished to a high shine. Along one wall, clusters of balloons were anchored over tables that groaned under the weight of their treasures. One table held every imaginable kind of appetizer. Another held an ornate punch bowl and crystal cups. A third contained mouthwatering desserts. A dozen different varieties of cakes. As many pies. Fancy, bite-size pastries. Even hand-dipped chocolate truffles.

When Colin escorted Loretta and Lizbeth into the room, heads turned, and there was a sudden silence, before voices began to murmur.

"Wow." Amy Mullins, the girl who worked in the cleaners, came racing across the room. "Beth, you look…" Lost for words, she simply shook her head.

"She means you look hotter than a movie star." Billy Barton paused beside Amy, his eyes as big as saucers.

"Well. Thank you, Amy. Billy. Aren't you sweet." Lizbeth could feel her cheeks growing hot. To cover her embarrassment she said, "I'd better get over to the dessert table and see if they need any help."

Loretta tucked her arm through Colin's. "You go ahead, dear. Don't worry about my date. I'll take good care of him."

Colin patted her hand. "Would you like some punch, Loretta?"

"That would be nice." She waited until Lizbeth was out of earshot before saying, "But not just yet. What I'd really like to do is sit down now with my friends. I don't think you'll have any trouble finding women willing to dance with you. I see Alfreda and Winifred, the Lassiter twins, looking like they'd love to pounce. I'll have to remind them that you're with me."

He chuckled as he walked her to a cluster of chairs that were quickly filling up. By the time she was seated, the mayor gave his welcoming speech, and the band broke into the first song of the evening.

Within minutes the dance floor was filled with couples.

Loretta touched a hand to Colin's. "I'll take that punch now, if you don't mind."

Colin excused himself and started toward the opposite side of the room, hoping to spend a few minutes with Lizbeth before returning to Loretta. As he approached he saw her chatting with the minister and his wife. Before he could reach her side she was walking toward the dance floor with Reverend Watson, while his wife stepped behind the dessert table to take her place.

"Would you care for desserts, young man?" Mary Lyn Watson greeted him with a friendly smile.

He shook his head. "Just some punch, please."

"You're Beth's new boarder, aren't you?"

He nodded.

"Been hearing all about you from folks in town. The Yardleys are so pleased with the work you're doing."

"I'm glad to hear that." While Colin waited for her to pour, he saw a man tap the minister on the shoulder and cut in.

Looking slightly surprised, Lizbeth waltzed off with a new dance partner. No sooner had the music ended than another man stepped up and smoothly danced her around the room. But in no time yet another man cut in, and she moved off in his arms.

"I think you've forgotten something." The minister's wife touched Colin's arm and indicated the two cups of punch which lay forgotten on the table.

"Yes. Thanks." Colin threaded his way among the milling crowd on the dance floor until he paused beside Loretta's chair.

She was looking very pleased with herself. "It looks like our Beth is having a grand time."

"Yeah." He was surprised by the quick flash of feeling. Jealousy? Impossible. He'd never in his life been jealous of anyone. But right this minute, seeing the way Lizbeth was looking up into the eyes of a burly man who was built like a linebacker, he found his hand curling into a fist at his side.

Very deliberately he forced himself to relax. He sipped his punch, wishing for something stronger.

When the music ended he expected to see Lizbeth return to her position behind the dessert table. Instead she was surrounded by a group of men. One of them handed her a cup of punch, which she gratefully drank. Another offered her a bite of his appetizer, which she refused.

When the next song started, Colin set aside his punch and started toward her. But before he was halfway there, she was moving to the music in the arms of another man. Minutes later they paused, then she began dancing with Jack Nowack, her mail carrier.

He returned to Loretta, who seemed to be thoroughly enjoying the show. She looked up as he approached. "I think I'd like that dance now, Colin."

"All right." He offered his arm.

Loretta left her cane beside her chair and held onto him as he led her to the dance floor.

"It looks like our Beth is having the time of her life."

"Yeah." It occurred to him that Loretta was, despite her limp, an excellent dancer. "You're very good at this."

"Dancing?" Her eyes twinkled with devilment. "Or matchmaking?"

"Is that what you're doing? Matching Lizbeth with every eligible man in town?"

She looked up at him. "Is that what you think?"

"Wasn't that your plan?"

She merely smiled and executed a smooth turn. "It's a pity that young people are so dense. But I'm sure that sooner or later you'll figure it out all by yourself."

As Lizbeth and Jack Nowack whirled past, they were stopped by another man who neatly cut in. Lizbeth whirled past in his arms, and Colin heard the sound of her laughter, as light as an angel's.

He saw the smile on Loretta's face and leaned close. "It sounds like she's having the time of her life."

"Yes. Doesn't it?" She nearly laughed at the little frown line between his brows. Instead she sighed. "You know, when my Henry and I were younger, we loved to go dancing. I suppose it was because it was the one way we could have our arms around each other without fear of scandalizing our neighbors. There's just something about being young, and in love, and holding each other while swaying gently to the music.''

''Yeah.'' He glanced over her head to where Lizbeth's partner swung her out, then drew her back for a quick turn.

When the music ended he graciously asked, ''Are you up to another dance?''

Loretta shook her head and leaned heavily on his arm. ''I think I'd better sit awhile. But if you'd like to find yourself another partner, don't let me stop you.''

''Thanks.'' He helped her to her chair, then glanced around.

Lizbeth was already dancing with Bill Yardley, and Seth Simpson, the druggist, was making his way toward them. Much as he'd like to cut in, it wouldn't be polite until the older man had his turn.

Colin spotted open French doors and walked through them to find himself on a balcony. The music was softer out there; the air perfumed with spring flowers. Leaning a hip against the railing he pulled a cigar from his pocket and held a match to the tip. As he expelled a cloud of smoke he saw Lizbeth dance by. He really was happy for her. She deserved to be the belle of the ball. He only wished she'd glance his way once or twice.

He turned away to stare out into the darkness.

Who was he kidding? He resented every man who got the chance to hold her, to look down into her laughing eyes. And it wasn't just because of that killer dress, or that sexy body, though heaven knew they certainly had everybody sitting up and taking notice.

So why wasn't he doing something about it? Was he going to stand out here all night and act like some lovesick schoolboy? Or was he man enough to go after what he wanted?

He tossed aside his cigar and started through the doorway. The music was just beginning again. A low, soft, bluesy ballad. There was no need to look around for Lizbeth. She was heading directly toward him. When she caught sight of him her smile dazzled. "Loretta said I might find you out on the balcony."

"Yeah. I was just coming to ask you to dance."

"I'm so glad. I was just coming to ask the same of you."

He felt his throat go dry as she stepped into his arms. And then, as he gathered her close, he thought he saw Loretta clap her hands together.

He started to chuckle. "That old schemer," he muttered.

Lizbeth lifted her face, brushing her lips against his cheek. "What?"

"Nothing." His mind was wiped clean of every thought save one. She was finally here in his arms.

Moving with him. Her perfume filling his lungs. Her body imprinting itself on his.

He'd thought this was all he wanted. And it was. For the moment.

But if he didn't get her home and out of that dress soon, he'd go slowly mad.

Chapter 9

"Sorry I made you stay so late." Loretta sidled up beside Lizbeth and Colin, and caught hold of Colin's arm. "But I wanted the chance to visit with all the neighbors I haven't seen all winter."

Colin closed a hand over hers. "I understand."

She looked up at him adoringly as they walked out into the night. "I had so many compliments on my corsage."

She paused at the curb and waited for Colin to help Lizbeth into the truck. Then she allowed him to lift her up and settle her in beside her young neighbor.

"He's so strong," she whispered as he circled the truck and climbed in the driver's side. "Don't you just love a strong man?"

She assumed the little hum was Lizbeth's affirmative response.

"Wasn't this just a perfectly lovely evening?" Loretta drew her shawl around her shoulders as Colin turned the key in the ignition.

Beside her, Lizbeth was holding herself so still, so silent, she seemed to be hardly breathing.

Colin glanced over. "Stafford really knows how to throw a party."

"This is just the start of our fun." The old woman placed a hand over Lizbeth's. "Have you told him about our Memorial Day Parade?" Without waiting for a reply she said, "The whole town takes part. Girl scouts, the senior dance troupe, who call themselves the Guys and Dolls, even children on bicycles and toddlers in wagons, pulled by their parents. Everyone who can't walk sits along the parade route and cheers. That night there are fireworks in the park. And then there's the Yardleys' Fourth of July picnic." She seemed to have a sudden thought. "You will have their place ready for the fourth, won't you?"

"Yeah. I think it's a safe bet."

"That's good." She nudged Lizbeth. "Did you hear that? The Yardley place will be done in time for their party. That's a relief."

She saw the matching frowns on both Colin's and Lizbeth's faces, and knew they were counting the weeks they had left. She couldn't resist plung-

ing the dagger a little deeper. ''Summer will be
here in no time. It's a pity you'll have to miss it,
young man. There's nothing quite like summer in
Stafford. Lazy days. Hot, steamy nights.'' She
sighed deeply. ''How my Henry used to love summer nights. He was such a romantic.''

Main Street was almost deserted as they drove
home in the darkness. The old woman had lingered, talking and laughing with everyone she
could think of, even the members of the band,
who'd been packing up their instruments. And all
the while she'd seen, out of the corner of her eye,
the looks that passed between Colin and Lizbeth.
Oh, she knew that look. Could still remember what
it felt like to be young and in love, and desperate
to be alone.

And so she'd kept them, deliberately drawing
out the agony. She hoped one day they'd forgive
her. But with a timid soul like Lizbeth, it sometimes took a bit of prodding to get her moving in
the right direction. As for Colin St. James, she figured this extra time wouldn't slow him down at
all. Unless she'd badly misjudged that look in his
eyes, he was ready to devour her young friend in
one quick bite.

Oh, the thought of it had her touching a hand to
her heart.

They rolled to a stop in her driveway and Colin
walked around to help her out.

"Come on, Beth." The old woman caught her neighbor's hand. "Walk with us to the door."

Reluctantly Lizbeth climbed down and carried the cane and shawl, while Loretta leaned on Colin's arm. At the door the old woman paused to look up at the big, yellow moon. "Oh, look at the sky. Now isn't that a picture?"

Colin tilted his head back. "Yes, it is. But it's getting chilly. You'd better get inside."

"Are you sure you two don't want to come in for tea?"

They both shook their heads at the same moment.

Loretta opened the door and Brandi came rushing outside, meowing and weaving between their legs.

"You missed me, didn't you, old thing?" Loretta picked up the ball of fluff and rubbed her cheek over the soft fur. "You know, Beth, it's nice to have a pet waiting for you when you come home at night." She turned to Colin. "I've tried to talk Beth into getting a kitten or a puppy. But she's afraid she'll no sooner lose her heart to a pet than it'll run away like last time, and she'll be left even lonelier than before."

He glanced at Lizbeth. "Is that true?"

She shrugged. "I just don't want to mourn the loss of something that's so easy to lose."

"And so she'd rather not love at all than risk

losing,'' Loretta put in dryly. She looked up almost slyly. "Well, I suppose Brandi and I should say goodnight.''

She thought she heard twin sighs of relief.

Colin leaned down to kiss her cheek. "Good night, Loretta. Thanks for being my date tonight.''

"Oh, you're more than welcome. I was the envy of all my friends.'' She turned to Lizbeth. "And I didn't mind having you along, Beth. Though I did think it was rude of you to monopolize so much of my date's time near the end of the evening. All that slow dancing.'' She shook her head from side to side.

Lizbeth brushed her lips over the old woman's cheek. "To make it up to you, I'll bake you a loaf of my zucchini bread.''

"Make it two loaves and you're forgiven.''

"You drive a hard bargain,'' Lizbeth laughed. "But I'd hate to have my favorite neighbor hold a grudge. Two loaves it is.''

"You're sure you two don't want to come in for a while?''

Colin threw back his head and laughed before leaning close to whisper, "You are some piece of work, Loretta Mayfair.''

Her eyes glinted with laughter. "Indeed I am. It's what my Henry always said of me. And don't you forget it.''

"I won't soon forget." Colin caught Lizbeth's hand and turned away. "Good night, Loretta."

"Good night, you two." She paused a beat. "Pleasant dreams."

She stood in the doorway and watched as the lights of the truck receded. Then she nudged the door closed and, still smiling dreamily, made her way to her bed.

In the driveway of Stafford Cottage, Colin turned off the ignition before glancing at Lizbeth. "Well. Alone at last."

"Yes." The word was little more than a whisper.

He stepped out of the truck and walked around to open her door, loosening his tie and drawing it free before stuffing it in his pocket. Then he undid the first button of his dress shirt and took a long, deep breath of night air.

As Lizbeth stepped down he caught her hand and linked his fingers with hers. "Loretta was right. Look at that sky."

She tilted her head. "I don't think I've ever seen the moon that big."

He grinned. "I ordered it just for you."

She glanced over shyly. "Thank you."

"No, Lizbeth." His voice was low. "Thank you."

She arched a brow in surprise. "For what?"

"For this night." He led her toward the front door. "For allowing half the town of Stafford to watch while I held you."

"It was nice."

He paused with his hand on the doorknob. "Having everyone watch?"

She shook her head. "Being held."

"I could do it again." His smile flashed, dark, dangerous, as he led her through the doorway. "If you wouldn't mind having no audience."

She voice trembled, but just a little. "I wouldn't mind."

"Having no audience?"

She swallowed. It sounded overly loud in the silence of the house. "Being held."

His hand halted mid way to the light switch beside the door. He turned to her. In the spill of moonlight she had the look of a frightened doe about to bolt. She was holding tightly to the nosegay of roses, as though to a lifeline.

He hesitated, then decided to choose his words carefully. "I want to hold you, Lizbeth. More than you can imagine. But I'm afraid it wouldn't be enough."

"I..."

He shook his head. "I'm not willing to settle for a few chaste kisses anymore. I want a whole lot more than you're ready to give."

Her chin came up. "How would you know what I'm ready for?"

"And if we don't tread carefully here..." He paused. His eyes narrowed on her. "What did you say?"

"I said how would you know what I'm ready for?"

"I just thought..." He decided to start over. "Why don't you tell me."

"I want you to make love with me, Colin. I want you to hold me and kiss me and make me feel like—" she took in a deep breath "—like I'm special."

"You are special, Lizbeth." He started to touch her, then thought better about it. Not yet. There were things he needed to say. If he touched her, he'd be sidetracked. Touching her had that effect on him, wiping his mind clean of all thought except one. "You're the finest, sweetest woman I've ever met. And I want, more than anything in this world, to lie with you. To love you. But I'm afraid."

"You, Colin?" Her eyes widened in disbelief. She saw him as utterly fearless. "Afraid of what?"

"Of hurting you. Don't you see?" He lifted a hand to her face, then quickly withdrew it. He wouldn't touch her yet. Couldn't. He needed a clear head. "I want you so badly, I'm not sure I can give you what you need."

At his admission she felt a rush of adrenaline. "And what's that?"

"I can see that you're a woman who needs long, slow kisses, and soft, easy, civilized loving. You need to feel cherished. I'm afraid I'm so hungry I'll devour you. And that would drive you away."

Maybe it was the magic of the night. Or the dress. Or the moonlight. Maybe it was simply his honesty. Whatever it was that had taken over her usual reticence, she found the courage to set aside the nosegay on the hall table and take a step closer until their bodies were brushing. "You could never drive me away, Colin." She lifted her hand to his cheek. Just the merest touch of her fingertips across his flesh, but she felt him flinch.

"Couldn't I?" His strong fingers closed around her wrist, stopping the movement. His eyes were suddenly hot and fierce. His voice a hoarse whisper. "Right now, right this minute, I want to tear that dress from you and see that body that's been tormenting me all night long. I want to devour you, inch by tantalizing inch, and take you right here on the floor like a savage."

His honesty was stunning. It excited her to feel the unbelievable tension humming through him, where his hand was holding hers. She pressed her other hand to his heart. If possible, it was even more thunderous than hers. "If you're hoping to frighten me, it isn't working."

"Then you're a fool." He released her wrist and took a step back, determined that one of them should be sensible.

"I am. As big a fool as you, Colin." She stepped closer and framed his face with her hands, staring into his eyes. "I knew tonight, when I walked down those stairs and saw you watching me, waiting for me, that this was what I wanted. I saw the way you looked at me. As if I were a beautiful, desirable woman. And I found myself wanting to be."

She lifted herself on tiptoe to brush her lips over his. Against his mouth she whispered, "You're what I want, Colin. Only you."

For the space of a heartbeat he stood completely motionless. Afraid to move. Afraid to breathe.

His voice deepened with feeling. "I need you to be sure, Lizbeth. I don't want you living with regrets later."

"I've never been so sure of anything in my life. When you held me tonight, and danced with me, I never wanted you to stop. I want you, Colin. I want you to hold me and love me."

On the dance floor, he'd wanted the same thing. But when he'd managed to put a little distance between himself and Lizbeth, he'd convinced himself, on the ride home tonight, that he would take the high road. He would be cool and calm and detached enough to see her safely locked away in

her room. But that was before. Before she'd
touched him. And kissed him. Now that she was
here, offering him everything he'd ever wanted, he
realized that he wasn't some high-minded saint. He
was merely a man. With a hunger so fierce, he
could hardly contain it.

He did what any man would do. His arms came
around her, pressing her to the length of him, while
his mouth covered hers in a kiss so hot, so hungry,
she was nearly overcome with the heat.

"What you're offering me is more than I'd ever
hoped for. And I'll try to be what you need. But
be warned, Lizbeth," he muttered against her lips.
"Be warned. I'm just a man. A man with a fero-
cious hunger."

He could feel her trembling even as he drew her
deeper into the kiss. And knew that, for all her
brave words, she was terrified of what they were
about to do. What was going on here? he wondered. She was a beautiful, educated woman who
had traveled the world. She had to be close to
thirty. And yet she was as jumpy as a virgin. Was
it possible?

The thought had him clamping down hard on
his own needs. Hadn't he sensed that this was a
woman who needed tenderness? A woman who deserved easy, gentle loving? If it killed him, he'd
give her what she most needed. Perhaps it was
what they both needed.

Without a word, he scooped her into his arms and started up the stairs.

With a sigh, she wrapped her arms around his neck and buried her lips in the hollow of his throat. That was nearly his undoing. His steps faltered, and he had to pause to taste her lips one more time. He drank from them, long and slow and deep. Fortified, he continued up the stairs until he came to her bedroom. He nudged the door open and stepped inside.

She'd left the light on in her haste. The bed was piled high with clothes; the floor around it littered with shoes. He shot her an incredulous look. "The impossibly neat Ms. Sullivan leaves her room in shambles?"

"Only when she's been prodded by her neighbor to be something other than bland."

"Are you saying this is Loretta's fault?"

She put her hand over her mouth and giggled. It was such a wonderful release of tension that she laughed again. "I'd have never had the courage to wear this dress without Loretta shaming me into it."

"Remind me to thank her." He turned and carried her down the hall to his own room. He kicked the door shut behind him and set her on her feet. He saw her smile fade, and cautioned himself to move slowly.

He kept his hands easy on her shoulders as he

brushed his mouth over hers and allowed her to sink softly into the kiss. When he made no move to do more, she sighed and brought her arms around his waist.

"That's nice," he whispered against her mouth.

She lifted her head. "What is?"

He nuzzled her lips. "The way you hold me."

Pleasure curled along her spine. And though she hadn't intended it, she found a spot where his shirt had pulled away from his waistband and her fingers encountered warm flesh. She was jolted. But no more than he.

"That's even nicer." He nuzzled her cheek, her ear. "I want to touch you the same way, Lizbeth. Flesh to flesh." His fingertips moved ever-so-gently over the exposed flesh of her back. Hearing her sigh he drew her closer and covered her mouth with his. His hands moved along her sides, until his thumbs found the swell of her breasts.

He felt her flinch, but as he continued kissing her, soothing her, stroking her, she sighed and gave herself up to the wonderful feelings spiraling through her. Even when she felt his fingers tug the zipper of her gown and slide the fabric from her shoulders, she offered no protest.

"You have the most beautiful body."

"It's the dress."

"It isn't the dress I'm looking at, Lizbeth."

His hands cupped her breasts with such care.

And as his work-worn fingers caressed her flesh, her breath caught in her throat. Her eyes darkened. Feelings she'd never even known she possessed were tumbling inside her.

"Your skin is softer than silk, Lizbeth. And your eyes are so expressive. I love watching them. Watching you."

She could hardly speak over the dryness in her throat. "It's so hot. Aren't you hot?"

"Yes." He allowed her to tug his jacket free, and then his shirt. He smiled as she drew her hands back, afraid to touch him now that he'd bared his flesh to her. "I'm still hot, Lizbeth. And I'm afraid it isn't the clothes. It's you. Your touch." He caught her hand and placed it over his heart. "Feel what you do to me."

His heart was racing even harder than hers.

His body was so beautiful. Bolder now, she splayed her hands over his chest, glorying in the freedom to touch all that smooth, tanned flesh and those rock-hard muscles. His heartbeat went from erratic to thunderous, and she felt a thrill at the knowledge that it was her touch that caused it.

"Colin, I can hardly breathe."

He smiled. "Yeah. I know the feeling." He brought her hand to his mouth and she felt the way his breath came in short, unsteady huffs.

He nibbled her palm, her wrist, and felt the way

her pulsebeat leapt at the brush of his mouth against her skin.

She kept her hand there, loving the freedom to trace the curve of his lips, the strong, firm jaw.

He reached his hands to her hips, sliding the gown free. It drifted to the floor in a cloud of silk. He let his gaze move slowly over her.

"Why Ms. Sullivan. You're just full of surprises, aren't you?"

"Hmm?" She stared, puzzled.

"You really do have legs. All this time I'd been wondering just what you were hiding beneath all those long, ankle-skimming skirts, and it turns out you have these fabulous, shapely legs."

She gave a laugh of delight. "I tried to tell you."

"So you did. I need to see more of these." He slipped a finger under the waistband of her panty hose and tugged them down before pressing her to the edge of the bed. Then, kneeling in front of her, he stripped them away and trailed his fingers upward from her ankle to her hip.

"Colin..." She started to shift away, but his hands were at her shoulders, holding her still.

"Shh. Don't say a word. Just let me look at you." And he did, allowing his gaze to linger over the flare of her hips, the fullness of her breasts, in a way that had the heat rushing to her cheeks.

Still kneeling, he leaned close and drew her

down into his arms, pressing soft, moist kisses to her neck, her throat, where he whispered, "Some men have to make do with their fantasies. But you're better than anything I could ever imagine. My sweet, beautiful Lizbeth. You're everything a man could ever want."

He brought his lips to her breast, nibbling and suckling until her sighs became little moans of pleasure.

"Colin…"

"Are you telling me you don't want this, Lizbeth?"

For the space of a heartbeat he waited, afraid of what she might say. If she changed her mind now, he would surely die.

"Oh, Colin. I do. Please. Now." She fisted her hands in his hair, wondering how she could have lived so long without this. Without him.

He lifted her in his arms and lay her on the bed, then quickly tossed aside the rest of his clothes, leaving them on the floor with hers. But instead of taking her, and ending this terrible need in both of them, he lay beside her and drew her close.

"Do you know how you look right now?" he whispered. Without waiting for her reply, he stroked a hand over her face. "Like an angel. The most beautiful heavenly creature, with the moonlight spilling over you, washing that incredible white skin with a hint of shine. And your hair."

He tangled his fingers in it, reveling in the silkiness. "Like spun gold." His voice lowered, soothing, calming her ragged heartbeat. "I love the way it slips free of all its pins and simply curls, this way and that like some wild tangled vine. And your eyes." He pressed soft butterfly kisses to her lids, and then the tip of her nose, letting her slide deeper into a river of gilded pleasure. "Sometimes, when you're happy, they're the color of warm honey. But other times, when you're angry, they'd put a storm-tossed sea to shame. They reveal everything you're feeling."

She'd never had a man say such things to her. They aroused even while they soothed. "What am I feeling right now?"

"You're afraid." He stared deeply and realized with a jolt that it was more than fear. "But not for yourself. You're afraid for me. Why, Lizbeth?"

"I'm afraid…you'll be disappointed when…" She swallowed. "I'm not very good at this."

His heart nearly broke for her. But he kept his eyes steady on hers as he traced his fingers down her body and saw her eyes darken again. "I guess I'll just have to prove you wrong."

He whispered soft, moist kisses over her face, her throat, then lower to her breast, laving with his tongue until her hands fisted in the bed linens. Then he moved to the other breast, nibbling, suckling until she moaned and arched toward him. But still he held back, pleasuring them both as he took her closer and closer to the edge of madness.

She fought against it. Afraid of this pleasure, so close to pain. Afraid of this great terrible need that was building inside her. A need that had her trembling, then climbing, her body arching, then tensing.

He found her, hot and wet, and took her on a fast, dizzying ride that left her no time to think, to prepare, as he took her up, then over.

She felt her entire body tightening, shimmering, then exploding. She gave a whimper as she poured herself out, then fell limply back, stunned by the feelings still humming through her.

But he wasn't through with her. Greedy now to give her more, to give her everything, he took her on another roller-coaster ride. With such heightened sensitivity, her body responded instantly.

She was wonderful to watch. The way she forgot all her fears as she lost herself in the intense pleasure. The way her eyes glazed, then went almost blind with passion.

He knew he could wait no longer. This huge need, so long denied, was like a beast struggling for release. He'd kept it chained too long.

As he entered her he saw her eyes snap open and focus on him. He struggled to keep his movements slow, his thrusts deliberate, drawing out the pleasure until it was almost unbearable for both of them.

This new, more acute arousal caught Lizbeth by surprise. She rose up, wrapping herself around him, drawing him even deeper. She stared into those incredible blue eyes and for the first time, wasn't afraid of what he'd see in hers.

"Colin." She heard a voice, low, throaty, incredibly sexy, and wondered if it could possibly be her own.

Then she was moving with him, climbing with him. There was so much strength in her. Strength enough to match his. And energy, pushing, driving, propelling her higher, faster. She felt the shudders that rocked him in the same instant that she felt herself shattering. Together they stepped off the very pinnacle of a high mountain peak. And flew.

Chapter 10

They lay, still joined, their breathing ragged, their heartbeats racing. The weight of him was pressing Lizbeth to the mattress. She didn't mind. In fact, it felt wonderfully possessive to feel that hot, slick body imprinting itself on hers. He had his face buried in the hollow of her throat, causing a tingly feeling up and down her spine, especially when he spoke. His voice seemed to vibrate through her.

"You okay?"

"Mm-hmm." She found it impossible to say more. There was a lump in her throat threatening to choke her. And she was horribly afraid she might embarrass herself by crying.

"I didn't hurt you?"

She shook her head from side to side, causing him to prop himself up on his elbows in order to see her face.

"Are those tears, Lizbeth?"

"No." She blinked furiously and was mortified when a single tear coursed down her cheek.

He pressed his lips to the spot. "It's wet. And it tastes salty. You're sure this isn't a tear?"

She couldn't help smiling. "All right. Maybe it is. But I don't know why I should be crying. I felt like I was flying. It was...amazing."

"So were you." He nuzzled her cheek, her jaw, her throat. "I thought you said you weren't very good at this."

"I've never been before."

That had him chuckling. "I think I should be glad."

Her cheeks flamed. "I didn't mean... It's just that...I gave up trying. It's been years..." Completely flustered, her words trailed off. But a moment later she ran a tentative fingertip across his shoulder. "Colin?"

"Hmm?"

"Was I? Good, I mean."

Laughter rumbled deep in his chest. "Are you fishing for compliments, Ms. Sullivan?"

"Of course not. But I need to know. Was I good? Or was I just...?"

"You were incredible."

"You're not just saying that?" Nerves had her running her index finger around and around the crisp dark hair that curled on his chest. She wasn't even aware of what she was doing.

But Colin was. "I'm not just saying it to hear myself talk. I mean it. But I think you'd better be warned. If you don't stop doing what you're doing, you may have the chance to find out for yourself very soon. You're getting me in the mood for an instant replay."

"But we just…" She saw the way his eyes darkened at her touch. "Could you…? Could we?"

"Want to find out?" He gave her a smile that had her heart doing somersaults. "Just keep that up, lady."

She couldn't seem to stop herself. She lifted both hands to his shoulders, marveling at their width. For so long she'd wanted to touch him like this. And now it was the most wonderful feeling to know that she was free to do whatever she pleased. She began tracing the muscles of his arms, trailing a fingertip along the fine dark hair that grew there.

She could feel him growing hard inside her. Her eyes widened with the knowledge that it was her touch that was arousing him. Hers. Her body that he craved.

Drunk with her newly-discovered power, she

sighed and brushed her lips over his chest and thrilled to his moan of pleasure.

"I warned you, Lizbeth." His words were a growl against her ear, sending shivers of delight along her spine. "I've wanted you for so long, I'm like a starving man at a banquet. Now there's no stopping me."

"Oh, Colin." She fisted her hands in his hair and arched up to meet him. "I'm so glad. Take me again. Right now. I want to fly."

"We should try to sleep." Colin lay with one arm under his head, the other cradling Lizbeth against him. They were both pleasantly sated. "It's been hours."

"I know." She pressed a kiss to his throat. "But I'm afraid to close my eyes. Afraid I'll wake up and find this was all a dream."

"If it was, we dreamed it together." He bent his face to her hair and breathed her in. There was such sweetness here. And so much innocence. And something else. A hint of long-buried pain. Even now, after hours of loving and laughing and sighing together, she was such a mystery to him. He wanted to know her. The child she'd been. The people who had helped shape the woman she'd become. "Tell me about your childhood."

"Why?" She looked up at him, all big eyes and wide smile.

"Because I want to know everything about you. What games you played. What foods you liked. What dreams you had for the future."

"My favorite food was a chocolate soufflé that our chef used to make in our Paris hotel whenever I'd come home from boarding school. It was a special treat he made just for me." She flushed. "That's why, in photos of me with my sisters, you'll recognize me as the plump one."

"Then it must be true what they say about beauty." He gave her an admiring glance. "In the eye of this beholder, I'd call you as close to perfection as a woman can get."

She felt herself glow under the warmth of his praise. "I have to say that I was relieved when some of my baby fat disappeared, and a few womanly curves appeared."

"I've had many an occasion to admire those womanly curves." He grinned. "What was your favorite toy?"

"An elaborate playhouse my Grandpa Sully had made for my sisters and me the year we lived in Switzerland." She laughed, remembering. "My older sister, Alex, hated it. She was always more interested in skating, or skiing, or climbing mountains with the Van Dorn brothers. And my younger sister, Celeste, never went near it, either. She preferred reading a book, or going to the museum with our mother, who was obsessed with art." She sat

up, suddenly animated. "So I had the playhouse to
myself. And because we were always living in hotels, that fantasy home became my real home."

"Did you ever live in a real house?"

She shook her head. "We've lived in castles,
inns, villas. And dozens of hotels. But until Stafford Cottage, I'd never had a real home."

"Now you have your very own grown-up playhouse." That explained so much. The love she lav-
ished on each little thing. The paint and wallpaper.
The furnishings. The yard. The gardens.

Lizbeth nodded. "Grandpa Sully offered to buy
it and incorporate it into our chain. That would
have relieved me of the financial burden. But it
would mean that it wouldn't really be mine. It
would belong to the stockholders. And if it should
show a loss for too many seasons, it could be sold
without my permission. Not that Grandpa Sully
would ever do that. But it was a possibility. So I
refused, and bought it on my own."

He arched a brow. She may call herself timid,
but she'd taken a giant leap, without the safety of
a net to catch her if she should fall. "That's quite
a risk. I'm impressed."

"Don't be." She sighed. "Every day I question
whether I did the right thing. I worry about paying
off the mortgage. Making repairs. Replacing the
ancient furnace, the plumbing."

"But look at you. You're still here. And you've

turned this into a charming, beautiful home filled with all the things you love.''

She nodded solemnly. ''I realized that the only way I was ever going to have the home of my dreams was to make it for myself.''

Did she have any idea what she'd just revealed? There was such sadness in her eyes. Such a hungry yearning for the one thing she'd always been denied.

He found himself wanting, more than anything in the world, to give her all the things she'd always craved. To make her feel loved and cherished and protected. But all he had to give her was himself. And so, as he brought his lips to hers, he kept his hands gentle, because that was what she most needed. He lingered over the kiss, allowing her to sink slowly, deeply, into the passion. He reveled in the taste of her, the texture. His hands moved slowly over skin as smooth as cream.

He allowed her to set the pace. Slow. Unhurried. He took his time, combing his fingers through the golden tangles that spilled over his pillow. Brushing kisses over skin gilded by moonlight. Staring deeply into eyes that reflected the light of a thousand stars in a velvet night.

She could feel the change in him and responded to it. This was a different sort of passion than the wild frenzy that had gripped them earlier and had driven them to a sort of madness. Now they were free to touch, to taste, to explore for as long as they wanted. To drift on a cloud of contentment, knowing they had all the time in the world.

Held in the grip of such tenderness, her natural shyness disappeared. She was free to explore his body as he explored hers. And she did. She was able to kiss him whenever, wherever she pleased. And did. And all the while she floated in a river of such sweet delights.

The scrape of his work-roughened hands on her flesh was heavenly. But with each touch she felt her blood heating, her bones melting. Those soft, butterfly kisses that whispered over her skin were so delightful that she felt herself sinking deeper, letting go of everything. When he tugged at her lobe, then darted his tongue inside, she felt tiny quivers inching along her spine. Each kiss was like a drug, filling her with the dark, musky taste of him.

She could hear his breathing begin to grow shallow as he continued touching her, kissing her. Her own breathing grew more labored, and her heartbeat speeded up. The thought of where they were taking each other no longer held any fear for her. He was so tender with her. So patient. If she hadn't loved him before, it would have been impossible to shield her heart from such gentle, loving treatment.

It gave her such a thrill to run her hands over

his body. To touch him as he was touching her. Those broad shoulders. That beautiful muscular chest. The incredible strength in those arms. She could feel the way he held himself back, allowing her to take the lead.

When he nipped at her shoulder she laughed at the quick little thrill that shot through her. But when he lowered his mouth to her breast the laughter became a moan of pleasure.

Emboldened, she traced her hand down his body and heard his quick gasp of surprise. She pulled her hand away as though burned.

"No." His mouth was at her ear, his voice rougher than she'd ever heard. "Don't stop, Lizbeth. Touch me."

And she did, feeling a sense of such power when she felt him tremble. She was rewarded by a low growl of pleasure as he lowered his mouth to hers and kissed her until they were both shuddering.

He was still kissing her, soothing her, as he brought her to the first peak. But he wasn't finished. He wanted more for her. So much more.

She was dazed, her body humming, as he entered her and slowly filled her. He drew out each thrust, each movement, taking them to a new level of arousal.

It was a long, slow, stunning mating that had them holding on tightly as they soared. Against her ear she heard him whisper her name. Just her name, as though it were a prayer.

She thought it the most beautiful sound she'd ever heard.

"What's this?" Lizbeth sat up at the clatter of dishes on the bedside table. Outside, the dawn sky was rosy with the first streaks of light.

"Food." Dropping his robe, Colin slipped into bed beside her, loving the way she looked, fresh from sleep, her hair tumbling around her face and shoulders in a riot of curls.

She sat cross-legged in the bed and slipped into his shirt to cover her nakedness.

He held out a plate of scrambled eggs and toast. "After all that exercise, we both need sustenance."

"Speak for yourself." She took the fork he offered and tasted before glancing at him in surprise. "This is good."

"Of course it is. When a man lives alone, he'd better know how to cook for himself, or have a couple of favorite restaurants nearby."

"It can't be easy to work as hard as you do all day, and then come home to cook your own meals."

He spread jelly on a piece of toast and broke it in half. "Maybe not easy, but necessary." He fed her another bite before taking one himself.

"Maybe you ought to consider hiring a cook."

"You interested in the job?"

She laughed. "Only if you decide to relocate to Stafford."

He glanced over. "Now that I've seen the many pleasures this town has to offer, I'm tempted." He offered her a cup of coffee.

"Mmm." She sipped. "Careful. I could get used to this."

"Hasn't anyone ever made you breakfast in bed?"

She shook her head, sending golden curls dancing.

"Really? Then I'll have to do this more often. Even the cook deserves a break from routine now and then."

Lizbeth felt such a warm glow she could hardly speak. He sounded like a man who planned to be around for a while.

At almost the same instant she cautioned herself not to allow such a thought. All it would do was bring heartache later on. After all, sooner or later he'd leave her. Didn't everyone? Isn't that the way life was?

She wouldn't think about that right now. It would only spoil everything. She'd already made her choice. For whatever time they had together, she was going to simply enjoy herself. And let the end of this, no matter how unhappy it might be, play itself out.

"Where did you go just now?" He reached over and tugged on a strand of her hair.

"Sorry. Just a fleeting thought."

He was studying her carefully. "Not a particularly happy one, it seems."

She felt the curl of pleasure as he played with her hair. Her smile was back. "How could I be anything but happy on this fabulous morning?"

How indeed? And yet he'd seen a flash of pain in those eyes. And found himself wondering what had caused it.

He took the empty plate from her hands. "Had enough?"

"That depends. Are you talking about food? Or something else?"

Surprised at her sudden boldness he laughed and drew her close for a long, lingering kiss. "I'd better be careful. You're getting to know me too well."

"I'd like to know you a lot more, Colin."

"Well then, why don't we begin with this?" He slid his shirt from her shoulders before drawing her down against the pillows. Then he kissed her until she was sighing.

Suddenly the sighs turned to gasps of pleasure as, with hands and teeth and tongue, he took her to places she'd never been.

Chapter 11

"I can't believe it's almost dinnertime." Lizbeth was dressed in a lovely, ankle-skimming skirt of pink and mauve swirls, topped by a mauve sweater with mother-of-pearl buttons. Her hair fell soft and loose, tucked up on one side with a pearl-trimmed comb. At her throat was a strand of her grandmother's pearls. She followed Colin down the stairs. "And we're just getting out of the bedroom."

"Yeah. I'm really shocked at your behavior, Ms. Sullivan." At the bottom of the stairs he caught her hand and linked her fingers with his. "Keeping me in bed for nearly twenty-four hours. And then forcing me to scrub your back in the shower."

"You have a very light touch, by the way."

He grinned and lifted her hand to his lips. "Thank you. I aim to please. But I'll remind you that next time it's your turn. And I don't want you using one of those sissy girlie poufs on my back. I prefer plain old soap and a wash cloth."

"You'll take whatever I feel like giving."

He stopped at the door and turned, hauling her into his arms. Against her lips he murmured, "You got that right, Ms. Sullivan. And I do like everything you've given me so far."

She absorbed the quick rush of heat and realized that even after a night and day of loving, he was able to melt her bones with a single kiss.

"And if I haven't told you yet," he murmured against her mouth, "I really love those girlie things you wear. Those soft clingy sweaters." He ran his hands down her back, up her sides, adding to the heat. Then lower, to her hips. "And those long, sexy skirts."

"You do? I thought you hated the fact that you couldn't see my legs."

"Yeah. I thought so, too. But now I've decided that they add just the right air of mystery. It's probably part of your devious plan to drive me slowly mad."

"Is it working?"

He kissed her again, lingering over her lips until she felt her blood heat by degrees. "You had me hooked with one look. And everything that followed was just foreplay, Ms. Sullivan.''

''Oh.'' She rolled her eyes in mock embarrassment. ''If only I'd known. I could have saved us both so much time.''

''Yeah. Not to mention frustration.'' He pressed his forehead to hers. ''If you had any idea of how much I was suffering, you'd have taken pity on me and ended my misery.''

''And why would I have done that?''

''Because you have a tender heart for all nature's creatures.''

''And you're definitely one of nature's finer ones.''

He grinned. ''Thanks. I think. Now.'' He turned and opened the door. ''Come on. I'm taking you to dinner.''

''Where?'' She followed him out on the porch and down the steps. ''The Village Pub?''

''Not this time.'' He unlatched the gate and waited until she'd walked out, then closed it behind him. ''I noticed a little Italian café and thought we'd give it a try. Have you ever eaten there?''

She nodded. ''They have great food. And I'm crazy about Italian.''

''Good. Me, too.'' Instead of catching her hand, he draped an arm around her shoulders.

As they made their way along the lane it occurred to Lizbeth that it felt so easy and comfortable to be walking like this. As though they'd always been together. Scant days ago she'd have been embarrassed to have her neighbors see her in such an intimate pose. But right now, this minute, she wanted to shout her joyful news to anyone who would listen.

Could they see it in her eyes? she wondered. She waved to the Lassiter twins, Alfreda and Winifred, who sat together on their front porch. They waved back, then bent their heads together, obviously excited to have something new to talk about.

She called out a greeting to Seth Simpson as he jogged past, huffing and sweating. He nearly stopped in his tracks. But to his credit, he managed to keep going, though he'd clearly lost his stride.

She smiled at Vicky Carter, the grocery cashier, who was just stepping out of the Main Street movie theater with Amy Mullins, who worked in the cleaners. The two returned her smile, before turning to watch as she and Colin strolled past.

If Colin was aware of their reaction, he seemed not to notice. "Here we are." As soon as he opened the door of Villa d'Italia, he breathed in the delightful perfume of garlic and spices.

The dining room had been decorated like someone's cozy, comfortable home, with framed wedding photos on the walls, and lace curtains at the windows. The lighting was dim. The music of a mandolin played softly in the background.

A pretty, dark-haired hostess led the way to a private booth in a corner of the room. A candle, placed in an empty wine bottle, flickered invitingly.

Colin ordered their drinks, then caught Lizbeth's hand between both of his. "What do you feel like eating?"

"Pasta." She said it instantly, without any hesitation. "A mountain of it. Smothered in meat sauce."

"You're hoping to load up on carbohydrates, aren't you?"

She laughed. "Am I that obvious?"

"Uh-huh." He lifted her hand to his lips. "Not that I'm complaining. I want you to have lots of energy. I've got plans for later tonight."

She looked up into those laughing blue eyes. "Sounds interesting."

"Oh, I think you'll be entertained." He kept her hand imprisoned in his while the waiter opened a bottle of wine and poured two glasses.

When they were alone again Colin touched the rim of his glass to hers. "Here's to us, Lizbeth."

"Us." Her eyes were as soft as her voice. "I like the sound of that."

"So do I."

They sipped.

Colin winked. "Though we really ought to drink

to Loretta Mayfair. After all, she did everything she could to get us together."

Laughing, Lizbeth touched her glass to his. "Then here's to Loretta."

"And to red dresses," he added. "I like them on you. And off you, as a matter of fact."

They were both laughing when the waiter returned to take their order.

"The lady would like a mountain of pasta smothered with meat sauce." Colin handed over the menu and added, "I think I'd like the same."

"You won't regret it. We consider our pasta at Villa d'Italia a feast." The waiter walked away, recognizing their desire to be alone.

"I remember the pasta and sauces of Sicily." Colin sipped his wine. "So different from the taste in Rome."

"Have you lived in both places?"

He nodded. "There was a U.S. base in Sicily. My father was commander there for a couple of years."

"Did you and your sister go to American schools?"

"For the most part. They always made American schooling available for the children of servicemen. But often my mother would see to it that we attended local schools, so we'd master the language. She wanted us to get the most out of our travels, so we could learn about the culture and make friends with people other than ourselves.''

"She sounds like a smart woman.''

"She was.''

Was. Lizbeth looked up at the finality of that single word. "How long ago did she pass away?''

"It's been almost ten years now. Both my parents went down in a plane crash just outside Paris.''

"I'm sorry.'' She placed her hand over his. "It must be so hard to lose both parents at once, and to lose them so suddenly and tragically.''

"It was harder on my sister. Serena was still in high school. I was out of college by then, and traveling all over the world. I had no way to make a home for her.''

"Where did she go?''

"I think I once mentioned my aunt Betty. The one who used to bake the terrific date nut bread.''

Lizbeth nodded.

"She lives in Colorado and took Serena in until she finished high school.''

"I'm glad she had someone there for her, to give her a sense of her roots.''

He shrugged. "I guess it was too late for Serena to put down roots. When it came time for college, she chose the other side of the country and headed east. And even before she graduated, she started traipsing around the world again.'' He shrugged.

"Maybe being an army brat does that. There's just not that desire to settle down."

Lizbeth felt a little chill at his words. Was he warning her that he was doomed to be a rolling stone? She kept her tone light. "I guess it's the same for my family. My parents have been all over the world, wherever Grandpa Sully asks their help in taking over a new hotel or inn. And they never seem to tire of it. They love starting over in a new place."

"What about your sisters? Do they still have the itch to move on?"

She shook her head. "We're all so different. Once Alex took over my grandfather's old hunting lodge, she knew she'd found her life's work. She recently married the new chief of police in Snug Harbor, a former New York City policeman. They've found their own snug harbor. I doubt either of them would ever consider leaving."

"How about your other sister? Celeste, is it?"

She nodded. "I don't really know if she'll stay in Libertyville. Right now she's immersed in the challenges presented in making the Old Liberty Tavern a success. But she seems much more suited to Paris or Rome or San Francisco."

"A bit of a sophisticate?"

Lizbeth laughed at the description. "Much more than just a bit. She's so polished and perfect she puts the rest of us to shame."

He caught her hand and lifted it to his lips, sending the familiar splinters of fire and ice along her spine. "You're no slouch yourself, Ms. Sullivan. A woman who grows her own herbs, cooks gourmet meals and could teach a thing or two to most interior decorators."

She shook her head. "I can't hold a candle to Celeste."

He fixed her with that piercing look. "You can light my candle any time."

She laughed. "That's just because you're so easy."

"I am where you're concerned." He looked up as the waiter returned.

Through course after course they feasted. There was thick, homemade minestrone, served with crusty garlic bread. The dressing on their salads was so light, Lizbeth had to pause again and again, in an attempt to guess the ingredients.

"Extra virgin olive oil." She closed her eyes. Tasted. "Basil. Shallots. A dijon mustard, I think. And a wonderfully tart vinegar that defies description. I'll have to remember to ask the chef for the brand name."

Colin leaned close to kiss the tip of her nose. Her eyes shot open.

He grinned. "I love it when you talk like that."

"Really?" Her eyes widened. "You should

have told me that sooner. I promise you, tonight I'll bring my recipe cards upstairs to bed.''

"No need." He waited until the waiter removed their salads. "Just whisper a few ingredients in my ear and watch what happens."

"I can't wait."

His eyes darkened. "Neither can I."

By the time they left the Villa d'Italia, the sun had disappeared and the street lights cast a soft yellow glow over the town.

Colin caught her hand. "Good choice, Ms. Sullivan. That spaghetti was the best. I'm feeling very satisfied."

"So am I. I couldn't eat another bite."

"That's too bad." He motioned toward the ice cream parlor. "I was thinking we could get a couple of cones for the walk home."

"Why didn't you say so? I always have room for ice cream."

They were still laughing as they entered the parlor and made their choice.

Minutes later they started for home, Lizbeth happily licking strawberry ice cream, and Colin indulging his love of chocolate by having three scoops, one of chocolate chip, one chocolate cookie dough and one double chocolate.

By the time they reached Stafford Cottage they were savoring the last bites. Colin unlatched the gate, and waited until Lizbeth stepped through, before closing it behind him.

"Let's sit on the porch awhile."

She nodded.

They settled themselves on the glider. It occurred to Lizbeth that it was so much more pleasant now that all the tension and discomfort between them was gone. She tucked her feet under her and leaned against his shoulder, loving the feel of his arms around her.

"Oh." She closed a hand over his. "This feels wonderful."

"I was just thinking the same thing. I don't know when I've felt more at peace." He pressed his lips to her temple. "This has been a special day."

"For me, too."

"I'm glad."

They sat in companionable silence, listening to the soft sounds of the night. The hum of insects. The call of a bird. An occasional note, pure and clear, of a violin.

"Where's that music coming from?"

Lizbeth sighed. "Loretta. Years ago she was a concert violinist. Her husband played the piano. Until Henry died, they used to give lovely recitals. Now, sometimes, she plays, though it's rare. She claims her fingers are getting too stiff."

They listened until the song ended. Then there

was no more music, and Lizbeth imagined the old woman putting away her instrument and carrying on a lively conversation with her cat.

A long time later, when the moon was full and golden, and the sky was awash with millions of stars, Colin stood and offered his hand. "Ready for bed?"

She put her hand in his. "I shouldn't be, after the hours we spent there. But the truth is, I'm tired."

"No wonder. We didn't get much time to actually sleep."

He held the door and they climbed the stairs together.

In the hallway he paused outside her door. "Does it still look like a disaster in there?"

She laughed. "I actually took the time to hang all those dresses and put away all those shoes and bags. Would you like to come in?"

"It doesn't matter. Your room or mine." He drew her close and kissed her, until they both felt the quickening of their heartbeats.

With her head spinning she caught his hand and nudged the door of her room open. "Then I choose mine. It's closer."

The little crystal clock on her bedside table said midnight. Lizbeth knew she ought to be asleep. But she was still too keyed up from their lovemaking.

She watched Colin in sleep, loving the way he looked, his hair so dark against the white of the pillow. His breathing so smooth and easy. Even in sleep he kept an arm possessively around her hip, one leg tossed carelessly over hers.

She hadn't meant for this to happen. She'd thought that she would be able to snatch a little happiness. That was all she'd intended. And why not, when he was so ruggedly handsome he took her breath away? When his kisses were so potent they could melt her bones and wipe her mind clear of all thought. But something else was happening here. She had seen it coming all night. All day. Sneaking up like a thief. And even seeing it coming, she'd failed to lock the door. And now she had no one to blame but herself for this mess. And it was a mess. Because, she realized, she'd never felt so happy, or so at home, with anyone in her life. She hadn't meant for this to happen. But it had. She'd lost her heart to Colin St. James. She'd fallen hopelessly in love with him.

She squeezed her eyes shut to keep from weeping. Oh God. What had she done? She'd never meant for it to go this far.

Chapter 12

Colin rolled over and reached out, eager for the warmth of the woman he'd held all through the night. It was strange how quickly he'd come to expect to find her there beside him. But the bed was empty. Disappointment washed over him. His eyes opened. Though the room was in darkness, he knew she wasn't there. Maybe because he'd developed a sixth sense about her. About the way she moved. The way she smelled. The way she tasted.

As his senses sharpened he could hear her moving around downstairs. He glanced at the clock and was relieved to see that he wasn't rushed for time. With his hand behind his head he lay back, sorting out his feelings. He'd come to Stafford with no expectations other than the opportunity to remodel a wonderful old house. He'd done this hundreds of times in hundreds of towns and cities. But somehow, in a few short weeks, everything had changed.

It occurred to him that he'd begun to think of things that would have once seemed impossible. Of sinking roots. Of making a home for himself, not in one of the world's great cities filled with classic architecture, but in the tiny town of Stafford, New Hampshire. When had this happened? And how?

The answer came instantly. The first time he'd seen Lizbeth. That first walk through this cottage. He'd felt...something. As if he'd come home.

He was an intelligent, sensible man. He may be a wanderer, but he'd never thought of himself as foolish or impulsive. But ever since that first day, when he'd come here seeking a place to stay, he'd had the feeling that he'd been meant to come here. And now, weeks later, he had an even stronger sense that he was meant to stay.

He slipped out of bed and headed toward the shower. As he passed the window he paused and opened the drapes. He felt his throat go dry at the scene unfolding below. With his hip against the sill he studied Lizbeth in her garden. What a picture she made, in one of those long, flowing skirts she favored, a bright yellow cardigan over her shoulders to ward off the morning chill. Her hair had already worked free of its pins to curl around her face.

He watched as she bent to snip a flower and place it in the basket on her arm. Her lips were moving. Was she talking to her blooms? He had no doubt.

With a smile he turned and made his way to the shower. He couldn't wait to get downstairs and taste her lips. Not to mention whatever it was that had those wonderful scents wafting up the stairs.

Lizbeth walked through her garden, still wet with dew, snipping fragrant peonies for a bouquet.

"Oh, you lovely things. One spring storm and you'll be finished for the season." Their heavy blooms would drop, she knew, petal by petal, over the ground, too fragile to endure the pounding of raindrops.

The earth was still hushed, barely awake. The sun was just beginning to peek over the horizon. The air was so still and silent not a blade of grass stirred.

"You're up early," she called to a robin, pecking through the grass. "I bet you have a hungry family waiting for you. All those little beaks to fill. And all hoping to be first."

Still smiling she continued on until her basket was filled with flowers. She picked her way through the damp grass and made her way inside, where coffee was already perking, and cinnamon rolls were cooling on the counter.

She had just arranged the flowers in several vases when she turned to find Colin standing in the doorway, watching her. For a moment she thought she detected an odd, almost pensive look on his face. Then he blinked and the look was gone, replaced by that heart-stopping smile she loved.

"You're up early." He took a step closer, still watching her. "I reached for you when I woke up, and found you gone."

"Did you miss me?"

He nodded. "I saw you in the garden. You looked so beautiful I almost ran down to join you."

"Why didn't you?"

"Because I wasn't wearing any clothes. I don't think your neighbors are ready for the sight of a naked man in your yard."

"You're right. Thank you for sparing them. And me. Though I must say, I don't mind the sight of you naked in the least."

He couldn't wait any longer. He strode across the room and gathered her into his arms. Against her temple he growled, "I really wanted to make love with you before I went off to work."

"That wouldn't leave any time for breakfast."

"I'd rather have you than food."

She laughed. "I'll remind you of that when you come in tired and hungry and there's not a thing on the stove." She lifted her lips for a kiss, then said, "Now come and eat. A working man needs a good hot breakfast to start his day." She lifted the lid on a platter to show him strips of bacon and a perfect cheese omelet.

He chuckled. "You're just doing this to make up for the fact that you weren't in bed when I woke up."

"Is it working?"

His laughter grew. "You do know the way to a man's heart, Ms. Sullivan. Is that cinnamon I smell?"

"Fresh cinnamon rolls. Come on. The table's set and ready for you."

She carried in the bouquet of flowers and set them on the round glass table set in front of the bay window. Then she left and returned with a serving table groaning under the weight of so much food.

"You don't expect me to eat all this alone, do you?"

"No." She poured two cups of coffee and took the place opposite him. "In fact, I've worked up quite an appetite."

"How long have you been up?"

"Oh, an hour or more." She served the omelet and ducked her head. Actually she'd been awake most of the night. But now, in the light of day, all those nagging fears seemed groundless. In fact, she had almost succeeded in convincing herself that she'd been a fool to lose so much sleep over this.

She was an adult, for heaven's sake. And enjoying herself for the first time in years. As long as no one got hurt, what could be wrong with it?

Across the table Colin sipped his coffee and watched the way she suddenly turned to stare out the window. Where had she gone? Wherever it was, it worried her. And that worried him.

"This is wonderful. Not that I'm surprised anymore. Everything you do is wonderful." He saw the way she forced herself back from that dark place inside herself.

"Thank you." She surprised herself by managing to eat quite a bit before she had to give up and sip her coffee.

When Colin had eaten everything she'd set before him, he sat back with a sigh. "It's a shame I have to leave for work. I'd much rather spend today the way we spent the weekend."

"It was grand." She stood and began loading the serving cart. When the table was cleared, Colin took it from her and pushed it into the kitchen. Then he gathered her close for a kiss. "I guess, whether I like it or not, I'd better go."

"Don't forget your lunch." She pointed to the thermal pack on the counter.

He hefted its weight. "What's in here?"

"Meatloaf sandwiches on homemade bread. A packet of fresh vegetables. A container of coffee. And chocolate chip cookies."

"You really think I'm going to eat all that?"

She nodded. "That day I visited the Yardley house, I saw how much hard, physical work you actually do. You could probably eat twice that much."

"One visit to my job site and you've got all that figured out?"

She nodded. Then a slow smile touched the corners of her lips. "I noticed something else, too. That tool belt you were wearing made you look really sexy."

"You think a tool belt's sexy?" He grinned. "Lady, if that's all it takes, I'll start wearing it to bed."

"Well, I wouldn't want to go that far."

"All right. Tell you what. I'll model it for you tonight. Right after you scrub my back in the shower. Deal?"

She couldn't help laughing. "Deal. But be warned. I intend to use girlie soaps and one of my shower poufs."

"That's all right. Once I strap on that tool belt, I'll be all man." He dragged her close for one last kiss before heading out to his truck.

Inside, Lizbeth watched as he backed out of the

driveway. That's what worried her. Colin was all man. So much so, she was beginning to lose her balance around him.

She set to work cleaning, scrubbing, scouring. She always did her best thinking when she was working.

"Hello." Loretta peeked through the screen door and saw her young neighbor on her hands and knees, scrubbing the kitchen floor. "Is that cinnamon I smell?"

"Loretta." Lizbeth stood and hurried across the room to hold open the door. Brandi rushed in, leaving the old woman to follow more slowly. "What are you doing walking all this way?"

"The doctor said I needed to stay limber. Figured, since I saw your young man's truck gone, I'd get a little exercise."

"Uh-huh." Lizbeth gave her a knowing look. "Is this the same woman who couldn't seem to take two steps at the dance without Colin's help?"

Loretta gave a throaty laugh. "There's nothing like the strong arm of a good-looking man to put a spring in my step." She settled herself on a kitchen chair and set aside her cane. "And your young man is particularly good looking." She cast a sly look at Lizbeth. "If you're of a mind to notice."

"Oh, I've noticed." Lizbeth moved around the

kitchen, putting the kettle on for tea, and setting several cinnamon rolls on a plate, which she set in front of her neighbor.

"I thought you might. Pretty hard to miss someone that rugged and manly." Loretta cleared her throat. "So, how're you two getting on?"

"Fine. Just fine." Lizbeth turned away and spooned loose tea into a strainer before setting it in a pretty little floral teapot.

"I never saw any sign of life over here yesterday. You weren't out in your garden. Never even picked up your morning paper."

Lizbeth held her silence while she poured boiling water into the teapot, then set it on the table, along with fragile cups and saucers.

"Strong and black, Loretta. Just the way you like it."

"Thank you." The old woman sipped, ignoring the fact that it was hot enough to burn her tongue. She'd spent a lifetime drinking tea. Loving the hotter the better. "Now about you and Colin. Did the two of you…strike sparks after you left me Saturday night?"

Lizbeth set down her own cup. "Are you asking me what I think you're asking me?"

"What I'm asking," the old woman said with a grin, "is if that young man was able to wait until he got you home before devouring you."

Lizbeth stared down into her cup. She knew that

sooner or later Loretta would pry it out of her. Besides, she was dying to tell someone. "We made it home."

"And then?"

"Colin was determined to do the noble thing and send me off to bed without so much as a good-night kiss."

"You're joking. After the look I saw in his eyes?" Loretta began to shake her head. "I must be losing my touch. I'd have sworn that he was about to gobble you whole."

"Well, that may have been what he wanted, but what he was determined to do was take the high road. And then, all his good intentions flew out the window. Thanks to that red dress..." She wagged a finger. "...which you shamed me into wearing..."

"Me?" The old woman looked as if she were about to deny, but Lizbeth cut her off.

"As I was saying. Thanks to that red dress, I was feeling quite unlike myself. And when he tried to be noble, I..." She fumbled for a word. "I...seduced him."

Loretta set down her cup with a clatter. "You what?"

"I told him I wanted him."

"Just like that?" Her old neighbor was looking at her as if she couldn't quite believe her eyes.

Lizbeth nodded. "Just like that. I don't know

what came over me. But I'm convinced it was the dress.''

''The dress.'' Loretta broke open a cinnamon roll. ''Of course, the woman inside the dress had nothing to say about this.''

Lizbeth fiddled with her teacup. ''The woman in the dress was feeling wild and impulsive and utterly free.''

''That's my girl.'' The old woman's eyes were shining. ''Now, isn't that the best feeling in the world?''

''I guess.''

The hesitation was quickly noted. ''And is your young man as strong and masterful as he looks?''

Lizbeth shot her a quick glance. ''Is that your way of asking me if we were good together?''

''What I'm asking is if he's strutting around like a rooster, and if you're purring like a kitten.''

''I guess….'' She blushed. ''Yes. To both.''

''Well, now.'' Satisfied, Loretta took a long drink of her tea. ''I'm glad to know that my faith in the two of you was not misplaced.'' She nibbled her roll. ''You know, Beth, you've been needing the attention of a good man for some time now.''

''Have I?''

''You know you have. It's fine, for someone like me who has lived a long and full life, to be alone. Henry and I had a lifetime to build the memories that still sustain me and give me so much pleasure.

But someone as young and vital as you shouldn't be spending your life talking to your flowers. Isn't it much better having someone around who can answer you? Who can finish your sentences? Who can make you laugh?''

"I suppose."

She saw the way Lizbeth was chewing on her lip. "Having regrets?"

Suddenly all the fears that had been building up throughout the long night threatened to erupt in a torrent. "Oh, Loretta. It wasn't supposed to be like this."

Helpless, the old woman shuffled around the table and gathered her young friend into her arms. "Like what, Beth? Come on. You know you can tell me."

"I know." Lizbeth had to make a supreme effort to hold back the tears. For she had vowed to never cry over a man again. Her entire body was rigid with the effort to remain in control. "You...know about what happened to me before..."

"I know, darling." Loretta patted her back and continued to hold her. "I've always been proud of the fact that you trusted me enough to confide in me. I like to think I've taken your grandmother's place."

"You have, Loretta. And I'm grateful to you for listening without judging me. But now..." She took a deep breath and pushed herself free of the comfort her old friend offered. "I thought... That is, I'd hoped..."

"That you could just relax and have a little harmless fun."

Lizbeth nodded and closed her eyes a moment, fighting to remain in control of her emotions.

"And now?" Loretta prodded.

"I think..." Lizbeth took a deep breath and decided to say it as quickly as possible. Maybe then it wouldn't hurt so much. "I think I'm in love with Colin. I didn't mean to, but it just happened."

"Love." The old woman caught her by the shoulders and held her a little away. "So that's the way it is."

Lizbeth nodded.

"And now you're thinking about all the things you ought to confide in the man you love."

Again a quick nod, while the tears that had threatened were put firmly away, never to be shed.

"Well now." Loretta caught her young neighbor's hand and squeezed. "Since you once confided in me like your grandmother, I'm going to give you the advice I think your own grandmother would give if she were here. A big part of love is trust."

"But..."

She touched a finger to Lizbeth's lips. "I know. Once burned. But Beth, honey, you have to learn to trust again. If this young man shares your feelings, he'll hear the truth and help you move on with your life. A life you can then live together.''

''But what if I'm just…convenient? What if he's the one who moves on? Without me.''

''That's always a possibility. And that's the risk one must take. If that turns out to be the case, you'll be hurt. But at least you'll know the truth.''

''The truth.'' Lizbeth closed her eyes. ''Maybe I don't want truth. Maybe he doesn't either. Maybe what he's looking for is just a lovely fantasy until he leaves here in a few weeks.''

''And what are you looking for, Beth?''

Lizbeth gave an expressive shrug of her shoulders. ''I don't know.''

''Yes, you do.'' The old woman placed her gnarled hands on either side of Lizbeth's face and lifted it. ''You want what everyone wants. One great love that lasts a lifetime. Happily ever after. And you can have it, darling. You're stronger and smarter than you give yourself credit for being.''

''How would you know that?''

She smiled. ''Because when I look at you, I see that girl in the red dress. That brave, fiery, fearless girl who knows what she wants and is willing to work for it. Or even fight for it, if necessary. She's always been there, Beth. But you've been busy trying to cover her up.''

''Oh, Loretta.'' Lizbeth gave a long, deep sigh and wiped a single drop of moisture that clung to her lash. "I wish I could summon that girl to deal with this."

"You will. When you need her." The old woman patted her shoulder, then called, "Come on, Brandi. Time to walk home."

"You aren't too tired?"

"I feel like a spring chicken." She picked up her cane and started to the door, with the cat circling at her feet. She paused and touched a hand to Lizbeth's arm. "Trust your heart, darling. And trust your young man with the truth."

Lizbeth stood by the door, watching as the old woman started home. Then she returned to the table and began cleaning up. She worked mechanically while she mulled the words of advice.

Trust your heart.

She'd done that before, and where did it get her? Her heart broken, and her life shattered. She didn't think she was strong enough to take it again. Maybe she'd wait awhile, and see where this new relationship went. If it really was a relationship.

Calmer now, she decided to work in her garden awhile, before starting dinner. As she weeded and pruned, she felt her spirit restored. For now she would continue down the path she'd chosen, enjoying this newly-discovered freedom, but keeping the past firmly in the past.

Chapter 13

In the late afternoon sunshine Lizbeth hurried along Main Street, hauling her small two-wheeled tote filled with groceries.

"Afternoon, Beth," the Lassiter twins called out in unison.

"Hello, Alfreda. Winifred." She paused, waiting for them to catch up.

"Have you ever seen a spring like this one?" Alfreda, wearing zebra striped pedal pushers and a polka-dot shirt, paused to lift damp white hair from her neck.

Her sister, Winifred, considered the wild one of the family, was wearing an identical outfit, with her white hair tucked under a bright orange bandana. The effect was startling. "It's positively balmy. More like summer than spring. Don't you agree, Beth?"

"I do." And all the while she'd thought it was her sizzling romance with Colin that had brought on this unseasonable heat.

Lizbeth swallowed back her smile. Everyone she'd met today had talked about the weather first, before leading up to questions about her boarder.

"You know what they say about spring," Alfreda said pointedly.

"What's that, Alfreda?" Lizbeth waited, knowing what was coming.

"A young man's fancy ofttimes turns to thoughts of..."

"...love," Winifred finished for her twin in a breathless voice.

"I hear tell the Yardley place is almost finished." Alfreda nudged her sister. "We happened by there yesterday. So many muscular workmen, sister and I couldn't make up our minds which ones to pick."

"Pick?"

"For next year's Spring Fling." Winifred lowered her voice. "We're not about to let Loretta Mayfair have all the fun. Coming in on the arm of that handsome boarder of yours. Having him fetch her punch and cookies every time she fancied some. Even dancing with him. Oh, no."

Alfreda chimed in. "She's not the only one who can snag a handsome escort."

"Of course not. Well, at least you have an entire year to make your choice." Lizbeth choked back a laugh and waved a hand. "Enjoy the sunshine, ladies."

"Oh, we will." The two old women hurried away.

All the way home Lizbeth couldn't stop chuckling about her visit to town. Everywhere she'd gone, the people had made pointed references to Colin. What a grand job he was doing at the Yardley place. How thrilled Bill and Sue Yardley were with the improvements to their home. How much the men of his crew respected him. And, from women old and young, there was always some breathless sigh or a mention of his rugged good looks.

And why not? Whether it was early in the morning, when he was still half-asleep, or late evening, after a full day of work, he never failed to stir her senses. He had, quite simply, begun to fill her life in a way that no one else ever had. And that bothered her more than she cared to admit. She could feel all her hard-earned independence beginning to slip a notch. And it was getting harder and harder to remain cautious. Whenever he held her, and loved her, she wanted to simply throw caution to the wind and declare her true feelings for him. But the fear that he might not share such feelings held her back. She would rather entertain her illusions for the short time Colin had left here in Stafford. Even if it meant their eventual parting would be quick and painful.

She unlatched the gate and started up the walk. At the sound of his horn she turned to see him just pulling into the driveway. He turned off the ignition and lifted his cell phone to his ear. Seeing that he was engaged in an animated conversation, she waved and continued on up the walk.

A short time later, as she was putting away the last of the groceries, he walked into the kitchen.

"My sister just called."

"All the way from Hawaii?" She pressed a lever and folded up her cart, stashing it in a storage closet.

"No. She and her husband are in Boston. Since Gary has to be there for a couple of days on business, she thought she'd fly up for a quick visit. I said I'd see if you could put her up."

"Of course. I'd love to."

"You don't mind?"

"Mind? Colin, even if she weren't your sister, I wouldn't mind. This is what I do."

"I know. But it means more work for you."

"I thrive on work."

"So I've noticed. I'll call and see if she can arrange a quick flight tomorrow."

"Oh, it'll be so nice for you to have a visit."

He grinned. "Yeah. It's been almost a year. I miss her." He drew Lizbeth close and buried his lips in her hair. "And I missed you all day. Want to scrub my back in the shower?"

"I think I'd better pass that up and get dinner started."

"Forget dinner." He kissed her hard and quick. "Let's shower together and then we'll walk down to the Pub."

When she hesitated he added, "You can cook tomorrow night and impress Serena with your talents. Come on. The cook hasn't had a night off since last weekend. And I'll give you another lesson in virtual auto racing."

"All right." She laughed as he pulled her along toward the stairs. "But you're going to smell like my girlie soap again when I'm through with you in the shower."

He gave a mock sigh. "Ah, the sacrifices I'm forced to make."

Lizbeth arranged a tall vase of deep purple irises and set it at the foot of the stairs. Then she stood back, considering. Maybe she'd put it in the guest room instead. She was halfway up the stairs when she decided she really wanted to set it in the middle of the dining room table.

That done she checked the appetizers she'd pre-

pared and began arranging them on a tray. When
they were just the way she wanted them, she carried the tray to the library and glanced at the clock.
There was just time to fill the crystal bucket with
ice, and chill some champagne, in case Colin's sister preferred that to wine.

A short time later, when she heard the sound of
Colin's horn, she ran her damp palms over her skirt
before hurrying to the front door.

"Serena." Colin was smiling broadly as he led
the way inside. "This is Lizbeth Sullivan."

He lowered a hand to Lizbeth's shoulder and
kept it there as he said, "My sister, Serena."

"Hi, Lizbeth." The young woman stuck out her
hand. "Colin says you don't mind me imposing
like this."

"It's not an imposition." Lizbeth caught Serena's hand between both of hers and studied the
tanned, dark-haired young woman who managed
to make a fisherman's knit sweater and khaki walking shorts look elegant. "Stafford Cottage has a
reputation to uphold, as the finest bed and breakfast
in New Hampshire. I'm used to finding guests on
my doorstep. I've never turned one away yet." She
studied Serena a moment. "You have Colin's eyes.
And the same smile."

"That's good." Serena glanced over at her
brother with a grin. "Then I guess we really did
have the same parents."

He winked at Lizbeth. "I used to tease her that Mom and Dad found her in the trash heap and only took her home because they felt sorry for her."

"I think I almost believed him. For about a minute. When I was five or six."

Lizbeth glanced around. "Where's your suitcase?"

Serena shrugged. "I'm only staying overnight. Everything I need is in this backpack."

"You're kidding. Everything?"

She handed over the purse so Lizbeth could test its weight.

Lizbeth rolled her eyes. "Now I know you're not kidding. This has to weigh ten or twelve pounds."

"Twenty. But you ought to try carrying it through Logan Airport. Then you'd swear it weighs a ton." She gave an admiring look around at the gleaming floors, the sunlit rooms perfumed with flowers. "This place is really beautiful."

"Thanks." Lizbeth smiled. "Would you like to see your room? Or would you like something to eat first?"

"Eat? You said the magic word. I'll go for the food. There wasn't time to eat before heading to the airport. And I'm not too fond of airplane meals. Colin raved about your cooking all the way here, and I'm already drooling."

Lizbeth blushed, as much from the compliment

as from the way Colin was watching her. "I put a tray of appetizers in the library. And if you'd like champagne, there's some chilling on ice."

"Champagne." Serena caught her brother's arm. "Come on. Feed me and ply me with champagne. And then you can tell me everything you've done in the past year. I'll give you five minutes before it's my turn to talk."

They were both laughing as they walked away.

"Gary really wants to save enough to buy a boat like the one we'll be working on." Serena was seated at the round glass dining table, enjoying her third helping of pot roast with mashed potatoes, gravy and tiny garden peas.

She'd been eating steadily since devouring the entire tray of appetizers in the parlor.

Lizbeth found herself wondering how someone so thin could put away that much food. She was glad now that she'd decided on comfort food, instead of the gourmet meal she'd originally planned.

Colin studied his sister over the rim of his coffee cup. "Isn't he going to put the two of you into a lot of debt?"

"Yeah. But it's what we both want, and we're willing to work for it." Serena polished off another roll and glanced at Lizbeth. "Did you bake these?" Without waiting for a reply she said, "They're wonderful. In fact, I haven't tasted any-

thing this good since I left Aunt Betty's. I hope
you don't mind that I'm making a pig of myself.''

"I love cooking for someone who enjoys eating
the way you do.''

"I don't always eat like this. I guess there's
never time. Gary and I are always on the run.''
She looked over at her brother, who was watching
her with a look of concern. "I know that look,
Colin. You're afraid Gary and I are going to bite
off more than we can chew.'' She swallowed and
chuckled at her pun. "But neither of us is afraid
of hard work. We'll get what we want, no matter
how long it takes us.''

"Okay.'' He leaned over to kiss her cheek. "I'll
quit playing the big brother act and let you and
Gary work things out in your own way.'' He sat
back. "Now about Aunt Betty. Have you contacted
her lately?''

"Whoops.'' Serena gave a guilty laugh. "I've
been meaning to, but I keep forgetting.''

"Then right after dinner I'll ring her up and you
two can catch up on a few things.''

She nodded and reached for another roll. "Okay.
Right after dinner. I promise.'' She looked over at
Lizbeth. "So, what's for dessert? Was that brown-
ies I smelled baking when I passed the kitchen?''

"It was. With ice cream and fudge sauce.''

As Lizbeth began to serve their dessert, Serena
touched a hand to her heart. "Brownies with ice

cream and hot fudge. If Gary was here he'd think he was in heaven. I don't think he's had a home-cooked meal since we got married.'' She glanced at her brother. ''With food this good, how do you manage to stay so trim?''

''I work hard. Remember?''

''Oh yeah.'' She grinned and dug into her ice cream. ''My poor big brother, raking in a fortune for simple little remodeling jobs.''

''If they were simple, everybody would be doing them.'' He rapped her knuckles when she started to eat his dessert as well. Then with a laugh he handed it over and shook his head in amazement as Serena cleaned the plate.

Serena wiped her mouth and set her napkin aside. Her tone grew serious. ''I know you're worried about the debt, Colin. And it's true that Gary and I figure it'll take us the next twenty years before we actually own our dreamboat free and clear. But we'll both be doing what we've always wanted. And to us, that's all that matters.''

''What about setbacks? Like illness?''

She shrugged. ''We'll deal with it.''

''What about kids? Have you given any thought to having a family?''

For a moment she looked pensive. Then she shook her head. ''We've thought about it. We'd both like to have a baby. But we're not sure it would be fair to a child to haul it all around the Pacific.''

''But what if it happens?''

Serena sighed. ''Then we'll deal with that, too.'' She gave Colin a wide smile. ''Want to call Aunt Betty now?''

''Sure. Anything to avoid my questions, right?'' He sighed. ''I'll get my cell phone.'' He turned to Lizbeth. ''Would you like to join us in the library?''

''You two go ahead.'' She began clearing the table. ''I'll just see to a few things in the kitchen.''

As they were leaving she called, ''If you'd like, I'll make a fresh pot of coffee.''

''Don't bother.'' Colin dropped an arm around his sister. ''I'd hate to see 'slim' here come apart at the seams. And I have a feeling if she eats or drinks another thing, that's exactly what would happen.''

Lizbeth was laughing as the two exited the dining room.

Lizbeth lay in bed, hearing the pleasant drone of voices drifting up the stairs. She had thoroughly enjoyed the teasing banter between Colin and Serena. Though they were often separated by thousands of miles, it was obvious that they had a deep and abiding affection for one another. It reminded her of the relationship she had with her two sisters. They were often apart, but the distances and the differences between them disappeared the minute they came together.

She'd been able to see another side to Colin tonight. The concerned big brother. It was obvious that he loved his sister deeply, and wanted only the best for her. But he'd wisely backed off from offering unwanted advice when she'd described the size of the boat she and Gary were planning to buy, and the amazing cost.

She yawned and closed her eyes, allowing herself to drift on a current of contentment. If she had a big brother, she'd want him to be like Colin. Likewise, if she had a husband, she'd want him to be like...

She felt the mattress sag, and strong arms slide around her, anchoring her firmly against a distinctly masculine body.

"Now who could this be?" she whispered.

"Hmm. That question could lead to all kinds of speculation. Such as, how many men in the town of Stafford do you allow to sneak into your bed at night, Ms. Sullivan?"

She pretended to yawn. "Too many to count. Dozens. Maybe hundreds."

"I see." He nibbled her ear. "And how many of them are allowed to do this?" He ran soft nibbling kisses across the back of her neck, along her shoulder.

She felt delicious tingles along her spine and shivered in anticipation. "Only a very special few are given this rare privilege."

"Only a few. That's a relief. Now I'll want their names in the morning, so I can see that they're run out of town."

"Can't stand the competition, huh?"

"You got that right." He turned her into his arms and covered her mouth with his. "I want you all to myself, Lizbeth Sullivan."

"Then you can have me." She wrapped her arms around his waist and snuggled closer. "At least for tonight."

"You're a generous woman." He nuzzled her lips. "And a very tasty one. Mind if I feast on you?"

"Careful." She breathed the words inside his mouth. "You're already curling my toes."

"That's nothing to what you're doing to me." He took the kiss deeper, as his hands began to weave their magic.

"I like your sister, Colin."

"So do I. In fact, I'm crazy about her. But I wish her room wasn't so close to yours. You know, I've been meaning to talk to you about that. It would be a simple matter to knock out a couple of walls over on the east wing, and turn those rooms into a master suite. Then you'd have your own private wing, apart from your boarders."

"I've often thought the same thing. In fact, I was hoping to do just that next winter. But if I'd done it sooner, this particular boarder would be very far away from my bedroom. And who knows if we'd have ever gotten together?"

"Hmm. Then I'm grateful that you didn't start your remodeling project sooner."

"So am I. But there's still the matter of your sister in the room down the hall."

He drew her close. "True. But right now I'm not thinking about Serena. In fact, whenever I get this close to you, I can't think at all." He rolled her over until she was straddling him. He dug his fingers into her hair, and moaned with pleasure when she lowered her mouth to his.

Against her lips he whispered, "Ms. Sullivan, you've got me so tied up in knots, I can't think of anything but you. I can't see anyone but you. And right now, I can't wait another minute to love you."

There were no more words as they felt themselves sinking into a deep, dark fathomless pool of passion.

Chapter 14

Colin came downstairs to find Serena and Lizbeth laughing together in the kitchen.

Serena was sipping coffee and nibbling a freshly baked banana nut muffin. She looked up at her brother's entrance. "I can't believe you've been eating like this every day since you arrived in Stafford."

"Yeah, it's a tough job, but somebody's got to do it." He paused to touch a hand to Lizbeth's cheek before pouring himself a cup of coffee.

The gesture wasn't lost on Serena. She arched a brow, and smiled to herself, happy that her brother had found someone so sweet and nice, even if only for his short stay in Stafford.

Lizbeth glanced at his clothes. "You aren't planning to work today? I thought you were only taking an hour off to drive Serena to the airport."

"I'm going to head over to the job and get the crew started before I pick up Serena. But since we're in the final phase now, there's nothing left to do but clean up."

"Clean up?" Lizbeth sloshed coffee over the rim of her cup. Very deliberately she set it down and dried her hands. "You mean the job is finished?"

"Just about. Bill and Sue Yardley may have a few last minute things they want changed, but for the most part we're through. I was hoping you could stop by later and see what we've managed to accomplish. The Yardleys are really happy with the results."

"Well." Lizbeth touched a hand to her stomach, where nerves fluttered. She'd known, of course, that he was very close to the end of this job. But she hadn't allowed herself to think about it. Nor would she now. It was too soon. She wasn't ready. "I'm sure Sue will want everything perfect before she starts showing off her new home. I think I'd better wait awhile."

"I don't know why you'd think that. Half the town has stopped by since we started." He chuckled at the thought of the parade of townspeople who'd come through the house since he'd begun.

"And no matter what the condition of her home, Sue always seems delighted with the company."

He motioned toward the platter of waffles and sausages. "Is that for us, or are you expecting company?"

"Oh." She managed a short laugh, though she was so distracted she could hardly think. "Go ahead into the dining room. I'll bring it along."

"I'll take it." Colin set the platter on the serving cart, before pushing it through the open doorway. He glanced over his shoulder. "Coming, Serena?"

"Yeah. I've been eyeing those waffles and sausages since I got downstairs." She trailed her brother from the room.

Lizbeth took a moment to settle her nerves before picking up the carafe of coffee and following them.

Minutes later the three of them were seated in the dining room. Lizbeth found that her appetite had fled. She merely sipped coffee while Serena matched Colin waffle for waffle, sausage for sausage, until the platter was empty.

"Why did you make so much food?" Serena groaned when she was through.

Lizbeth laughed. "For one thing, it's your last morning in Stafford. I wanted this breakfast to be grand. And the truth is, I'm rather amazed at how much you manage to eat. Besides, knowing how you feel about airplane food, I wouldn't want you to have to eat something during your flight. In fact, I intend to wrap the rest of these muffins so you can take them with you.''

''See how thoughtful she is?'' Colin drained his coffee, then pushed away from the table. ''I'll be back in two hours to pick you up, Serena. I think it's a good thing you're leaving today. A few more days here and Gary wouldn't recognize the little butterball getting off the plane.'' He bent to kiss his sister's cheek. ''Two hours. Be ready.''

''You're talking to a traveling fool, remember? I could be packed and ready in five minutes.''

''Yeah. I think you could.'' He paused to brush a kiss across Lizbeth's cheek. ''If you'd like, I'll stop by on the way home from the airport and pick you up, so you can see what we've accomplished at the Yardleys.''

She nodded. ''All right. I'd like that.''

When he was gone, Serena began stacking dishes on the serving cart.

Lizbeth caught her by the arm. ''Stop that. You're a guest here. Leave that for me.''

''You have to let me do it. I need to work off some of this food.'' Serena cleared the table and pushed the cart toward the kitchen, with Lizbeth trailing behind. ''Besides, Colin is right. Just one night here and my clothes feel snug.''

While she began loading dishes into the washer

Serena said casually, "Colin seems really comfortable here."

Lizbeth wiped down the stove. "He should be. He's been here for more than six weeks."

"To a couple of army brats like us, six weeks can be a lifetime. I'm surprised he's lasted this long. Usually after a month the walls start closing in and he has to hit the road again."

Lizbeth moved to the counter, spraying, wiping, trying to ignore the jittery feeling Serena's words were causing. "Colin told me about your childhood. It was much like mine."

"You traveled a lot?"

Lizbeth nodded. "All over the world."

"Oh. That explains it."

Lizbeth arched a brow. "Explains what?"

"The reason that you and Colin…that in such a short time you became so…easy with each other."

Feeling slightly uncomfortable Lizbeth tried to shift the conversation to something safer. "I was sorry to hear about your parents. It had to be hard, losing them both together, while you were still so young."

"Yeah. My aunt Betty was a lifesaver. But her feelings were really hurt when I went away to college. She just didn't get it."

"Get what?"

Serena shrugged. "What people like you and I understand instinctively. I couldn't stay there. It was this really neat old house in the heart of suburbia, with a big rolling lawn and all these big old trees. I was given my cousin's room, because she was already married. And the walls were covered with pennants and movie posters. My aunt cooked these enormous, wonderful meals. And every Sunday, after church, she had a bunch of friends over for brunch. She belonged to a book club, a quilting club and the local theater group. Day after day, week after week, nothing ever changed. We never did anything new or different.''

It occurred to Lizbeth that Serena had just described her idea of heaven. It was, in fact, pretty much a description of her life in Stafford.

She was startled when Serena added softly, ''I felt like I was suffocating. I had to get as far away as possible. And even when I started classes at Boston University, I had to keep moving. I spent a semester in Ireland, another in France. Poor Aunt Betty. She never understood.'' She sighed. ''I never thought I'd meet anyone who would understand my itch to travel. That's why I'm so lucky I found Gary. We met in Dublin, during a student project. Two years later we ran into each other in Paris. We carried on most of our courtship through the mail and the Internet. We were married in England, and spent the next year in Germany. Now we're off to Fiji, on the grandest adventure yet.''

''But where is home?'' Lizbeth asked softly.

Serena shrugged. "Home is wherever we happen to be at the moment. I guess you can understand such things. Home just doesn't have the same meaning for people like us. Like Colin and me, you've spent a lifetime on the move. A house and a yard and a picket fence might spell home to some, but to people like us..." She shivered in mock horror. "That spells prison." She turned away. "Thanks for letting me work off some of your wonderful cooking, Lizbeth. Now I'd better get upstairs and make sure my backpack is properly stuffed."

As she danced away, Lizbeth sank down onto a kitchen chair and stared at the back door. Was the sun still shining? She couldn't tell. Were the birds still singing? If so, she couldn't hear them. All she could see was Serena's smile as she talked about her freedom to travel the world. And all she could hear were her words, echoing in her mind.

A house and a yard and a picket fence might spell home to some, but to people like us that spells prison.

People like us.

But she wasn't like Colin and Serena. And never had been. She'd spent a lifetime traveling, and never feeling as though she belonged anywhere. Until here at Stafford Cottage.

She wanted to belong here. Wanted to sink down roots, and stay here until she was as old as

Loretta. This had become her home, her haven. And she'd done it alone.

If a man should come along who was willing to fit his life to hers that would sweeten the dream even more. She'd thought, hoped, foolishly perhaps, that man would be Colin.

Apparently she'd made a miscalculation. But it wasn't his fault; it was hers. Hadn't he been totally honest with her right from the start? He was an architect who didn't even own his own home. A man who slept in a loft in his office, so that he could be free to move on whenever he chose. And he'd be moving on soon, now that the Yardley project was completed.

He'd never said he loved her. Never suggested that they would have a future together. And certainly had made no false promises.

She couldn't find fault with his behavior. He'd never led her on. All he'd wanted was the here and now, and whatever pleasure the two of them could bring to one another. Hadn't she known as much? She'd walked into this situation with her eyes open.

Now it was time to face some painful facts.

There was no doubt that when he left Stafford her heart would be broken. But she'd learned that even with a heart shattered beyond repair, and dreams left in tatters, life goes on.

She stood and forced herself to finish her kitchen

chores. She'd need to put a good face on things when she faced Colin and said her goodbyes to Serena.

Goodbye. It was the word she despised above all others.

With the package of home-baked muffins balanced carefully in her lap Serena sat back. "I had the best time." She watched the small-town images move slowly past the truck window as Colin drove along Main Street. Toddlers on tricycles. Young mothers pushing strollers. Elderly couples strolling arm in arm. Business people exchanging pleasantries outside their shops. "And this has been a neat little place to see."

"Yeah. Stafford's a great place. I'm glad we had this visit."

"Next year it's your turn, big brother. I'll expect you to fly up to Fiji and fill me in on what's happening in your life. Promise?"

"You know I can't promise that. But I'll keep the option open."

She chuckled. "Do you know how long our family has been using that phrase? When we were kids, I remember hearing Dad say that to Mom. *I'll keep the option open.* But you're right. Who knows where either of us will be by this time next year? Gary and I will probably be somewhere in the South Seas, aboard our own boat. And you'll probably be in Rome or Venice, studying more of those dusty old palaces you've always loved.''

"Could be. But where I'm hoping to be is right here in Stafford."

Serena turned to him with a stunned expression. "Here? For heaven's sake, why?"

"Hey." He tugged on a lock of her hair. "What's the matter with you? You'd have to be blind not to see the way I feel about Lizbeth."

"Yeah. The two of you can't keep your eyes off each other." Or their hands, she'd noted. "So?"

"So, I want to be here. With Lizbeth."

She crossed her arms over her chest. "Oh, sure. For how long?"

"Oh, I figure a lifetime or two."

"You're—" she shot him a puzzled glance "—going to put down roots?"

"That's what I'm planning."

"Have you two talked it over?"

He shook his head. "I wanted to get this job done first. Then I was hoping to ease into something more…permanent."

He turned off the highway into the small airport. As he pulled up to the terminal and parked, he saw the stunned look on his sister's face. "Hey. I thought you liked Lizbeth."

"I do. She's the greatest. But…" She swallowed. "I think I may have hurt your chances a bit, big brother."

His smile dissolved. "How?"

She shook her head. "After you left this morning I went on and on about how we were all alike. Never wanting to be in one place for very long." She covered her face with her hands as another thought struck. "Oh no! I even compared a house and a picket fence to a prison. Oh, Colin. I'm sorry. I had no idea…"

Colin felt his heart take a sudden, hard, heavy bounce. He stepped out of the truck and circled around to help his sister down, using that moment to compose his features.

As he gathered her close she threw her arms around his neck and muttered, "Me and my big mouth. Now I've spoiled everything."

"No harm done, Serena." He kissed her, then stepped back. "Give my best to Gary. And send me a picture of your yacht."

"Yeah." She studied him. "You're sure you can patch things up with Lizbeth?"

"Don't give it another thought."

She turned away and hurried inside the terminal.

He waited until she'd gone through the security check. Then he climbed into his truck and drove like a madman. Wondering how in the world he could convince a tender soul like Lizbeth that a leopard could change its spots.

She wasn't in the yard. Not a good sign, he thought. On a day like this, he'd expected to find her talking to her flowers. But then, hadn't she agreed to go to the Yardley house when he returned? Maybe she was inside, waiting for him.

He strode through the kitchen and found it empty. The dining room, the library, the parlor, were just as empty.

"Lizbeth." He called her name as he started up the stairs. There was no answering call.

He knocked on her bedroom door. Hearing no response he opened it and looked in. The bed was neatly made. Not a thing out of place. A bouquet of fresh flowers on the night table. And no sign of Lizbeth.

He moved to his room, which was empty. The guest room where Serena had stayed was already spotless, the bed linens changed, the fresh flowers removed. The other guest rooms were all equally tidy, and empty.

Ordinarily he wouldn't have given this a second thought. After all, Lizbeth spent most days visiting neighbors, shopping in town, or running errands for Loretta. But knowing what Serena had told her, he felt a growing sense of unease. He had the distinct feeling that her absence had much more significance.

On an impulse he started toward Loretta Mayfair's house. If anyone in Stafford knew what was going on in Lizbeth's mind, it was that crafty old woman. And right now, he was desperate to find

someone who could steer him on the right course
toward winning her heart and hand.

Loretta looked up at the shadow falling over her
doorway. Seeing Colin, she spooned the rest of the
cat food into a dish.

"Well, Brandi." She ran a hand over the old
feline's back before straightening. "Look who's
come to call." She motioned Colin inside. "Are
you here to ask me out again, young man?"

"I was hoping you'd know where Lizbeth
went."

"Oh, darn. And here I thought I'd have a dinner
date."

Despite his concern, he managed a smile.
"We'll definitely have a date, as long as you give
me a rain check. Right now I have something
more important on my mind. Have you seen Lizbeth?"

"Matter of fact I have."

His sigh was audible. "Where is she?"

The old woman made a great show of turning
toward the clock on the wall. "I'd say right about
now she's midway between here and her place."

He shook his head. "I just came from there.
Wouldn't I have passed her on the way here?"

"Not unless you came through the back gardens."

He turned toward the door. "Thanks, Loretta."

"Just a minute, young man."

At the sudden change in her tone he turned back.

She sank onto a kitchen chair and indicated the other one across the table. "Sit yourself down a minute. There are some things you ought to know."

He sat and waited.

"Our Beth is a very special girl."

He nodded. "I know."

She looked at him a minute. Then she arched a brow. "Yes. I think you do." She thought carefully before saying, "Are you planning on leaving, now that your job at the Yardleys is over?"

"That depends on Lizbeth."

"You mean, if she asked you to stay, you would?"

He nodded. "In a heartbeat."

She sat back. A slow smile spread across her face. "Well, now. Isn't this interesting?" She reached across the table and placed a hand over his. "I'm not sure Beth will find the courage to ask you to stay. She's...been hurt."

"I know."

"You do, do you?" She studied his eyes, so blue they put the sky to shame. "How much do you know?"

"Not nearly enough. Enough to notice that she doesn't trust anyone or anything. But that's about all I know. She freezes up whenever I get too close. Can you tell me what happened?''

She shook her head. ''I could. But I won't. I have no right to betray her confidence. But I will tell you this. If you ask the right questions, you may get the answers you're seeking.''

''And you're not going to coach me on the right questions, are you?''

She chuckled. ''A smart young man like you will figure it out all by yourself.''

He stood and started toward the door. Then he turned back and caught her by the shoulders, lifting her out of the chair before kissing her soundly.

She touched a hand to her mouth. ''What was that for?''

''For being an incurable romantic.''

''It takes one to know one.''

She grinned at his retreating back. Then she hurried to the door and watched as he strode up the lane toward Stafford Cottage.

To her cat she muttered, ''Our Beth may think she's a timid mouse. But I have an idea that our young man is about to show her that she's made of better stuff than she thinks.''

Chapter 15

Lizbeth caught sight of Colin's truck and took a deep breath. She could get through this. All it would require was a smile as he drove her to the Yardley house and took her on a tour. In another day or two he'd be gone, and her life would return to normal. In no time she'd be caught up in the madness of tourist season, with no time to think of anything beyond the next meal, the next guest.

She squared her shoulders and stepped into the kitchen, expecting to find him waiting for her. Instead the room was empty.

She walked through the house, and was surprised to find no sign of him.

She was just climbing the stairs when she heard

the sound of the kitchen door closing. She paused with her hand on the banister. Turned. And saw him standing at the foot of the stairs.

"Serena wanted me to be sure and thank you for making her feel so welcome."

"It was easy to do. She's sweet."

"She talks too much." He was watching her in that quiet, intense way that always made her uncomfortable. "She told me what she said about houses with picket fences."

Her tone was pure ice, to cover the hurt. "I'm sure the two of you had a good laugh over it."

"I didn't find it funny. And when Serena realized what she'd done, she was sorry. I want you to know, Lizbeth, I don't share my sister's sentiments."

"She said the two of you are alike. That you've never been able to stay in one place for more than a few weeks before having to move on. Are you saying your sister lied?"

"No. That was true once. My whole life has been spent on the run. I've never had the urge to stay put until now. But that all changed when I met you."

She forced herself to meet his eyes. Her voice was cool, calm. "You don't need to do this, Colin."

"Do what?"

"Make pretty speeches for my sake."

He couldn't keep the anger from creeping into

his tone. "You think I'm just saying this to salve my conscience because I slept with you?"

"No. Of course not. You're a good man, Colin. But I suppose even the best of men are uncomfortable at the end of a pleasant affair."

"A pleasant affair." His eyes narrowed. "Is that all you think this was?"

"Of course it was. But don't worry. I won't hold you, or cling to you or lay any guilt on you by weeping. It's simply not my style."

"No. That wouldn't be your style, Lizbeth." He climbed the first step, his eyes steady on hers. "You'll just keep that pretty Mona Lisa smile in place, and keep all your deep dark secrets to yourself. You'll be content to let me walk away without ever telling me what's really going on inside your head."

She refused to squirm. Instead she gave him a measured look. "I have no intention of talking about myself. I'm not the issue here."

"No. The issue here is trust." He took another step toward her. "Somewhere along the line, someone betrayed your trust. And you were so damaged, you promised yourself you'd never allow yourself to be hurt like that again." His tone softened. "Don't you see, Lizbeth? Until you tell me what happened, I have no way of breaking through that wall you've built around your heart."

For almost a full minute there was no sound except the ticking of the clock on the landing. It seemed, for a moment, that Lizbeth was going to break down. Then she lifted her chin and gathered her dignity around her like a cloak.

"If you don't mind…"

"I do mind." He caught her by the arm. "Don't turn away now, Lizbeth. We need to…"

The ringing of his cell phone interrupted. He groaned aloud as he snatched it from his pocket. "Yes?"

He listened, then sighed. "I'll be right there."

He jammed the phone into his pocket. "Bill Yardley says the crew is finished. He wants me to inspect the job before he pays them. Will you come with me?"

She shook her head. "I can't. Not right now."

As she started to turn away he lay a hand on her arm. "I'll have to be gone several hours. But I hope we can talk when I come back."

Because she was afraid to trust her voice, she merely gave a slight nod of her head.

She stood where she was, listening to the sound of his footsteps and the closing of the door. Minutes later she heard the sound of his truck. And then there was only silence. It was a sound she'd lived with for a very long time.

Lizbeth knelt in the garden, pruning, snipping, weeding. The sun, which had earlier vanished behind clouds, was now shining brightly.

She needed this physical release to keep herself on an even keel. She'd kept her emotions bottled up so tightly, she'd feared they might soon explode. But now she was calm again. Calm and in control.

Control was so important to her. For a short time in her life she'd lost it. And because of that, she had been lost as well. But she'd found herself here, in this pretty little town, which demanded nothing more of her than she was willing to give. She'd found herself in this lovely old cottage, which had offered her so much more than just a haven. Here, while she'd spun cloth, where she'd knitted and crocheted and quilted, where she'd planted her flowers, and indulged in the simple things that nourished her soul, she'd also dreamed her dreams. If only a few of them managed to come true, that would be enough to satisfy her.

She heard the crunch of tires along the driveway and knew, without looking up, that Colin had returned. She continued weeding, while she mentally braced herself for another confrontation. This time she was ready. Armed with her dignity, she wouldn't be goaded into saying or doing anything that might provoke an argument. She would, by heaven, retain her dignity.

She heard the truck door slam shut. Heard the sounds of Colin's footsteps as he came near. She attacked a vine that had attached itself to the branches of her rhododendron, tugging until it was torn from the soil. When she turned to toss it into the wheelbarrow, she was startled to see Colin kneeling beside her. In his hands was a tiny ball of white fluff.

"What's this?" Her eyes widened. "A kitten?"

He nodded. "Now that they're old enough to be weaned, the Yardleys gave me my choice. It wasn't really any contest. This was the cutest one of all."

"She's adorable." Lizbeth ran a finger along the kitten's back and watched it arch upward. "What did you call her?"

"I thought I'd let you name her." He smiled. "She's yours."

"Mine?" She lifted her hand away. "Oh, no. I can't. You know I don't want... What if she ran away? Or got hit by a car? Or..."

"Lizbeth." He put a hand over hers. "Not everything you love is going to leave you."

At his simple statement she was too stunned to say a word. This wasn't at all what she'd been expecting. And now she was caught completely off guard.

She continued kneeling in the grass, her eyes a little too bright, while the kitten stood on its hind legs to peer into the watering can. The can toppled, spraying water everywhere. The kitten ran off, shaking its tiny body, before getting caught up in chasing after a butterfly.

Colin pressed her hand between both of his. "That is what happened, isn't it? Someone you loved left you?"

It was her intention to deny. To close herself up as she always had, in order to protect herself. But even as she started to deny it, she found herself nodding. And then, to her amazement, the words, so long locked inside, just tumbled out.

"At least I thought it was love. Now, lately, I'm beginning to realize I had no idea what love really was. It happened so long ago, it just seems like it was all a dream."

"Why don't you tell me?"

His voice was soothing. As was his touch. And it suddenly seemed the most natural thing in the world to share her story with him.

"I was eighteen. In boarding school in Switzerland. Alone, and miserably lonely. He wasn't much older, a student in a boys' academy nearby. But he seemed to be all the things I wasn't. Funny and irreverent. And ready to do anything on a dare. Looking back, I realize there was a desperation to his actions. A need to taste everything, try everything, as though time might be running out. But then I was too young to understand or to question.

I just knew that with him, everything was such fun.''

She darted a glance at Colin, then away, afraid of the disappointment she would see in his eyes. ''My parents had arranged that I would remain at school for holiday because they were starting a new venture and were horribly overworked. Neither of my sisters could join me because they had made other plans. Alex was going skiing in the Alps. Celeste was going to Rome with her art class. I was feeling desperately sorry for myself. And then, in the little Swiss village near my school, there was JeanClaude, also alone on holiday. He made me laugh. He took me shopping, and dancing, and that night, he took me to his room.''

She gave a long, deep sigh. ''We agreed to meet the following weekend, at the same room. When he showed up, he seemed pale. His humor seemed a little forced. But he said it was just a cold. And he knew the perfect cure. He wanted to marry me. I was a little horrified, but I was also thrilled. I'd never, in my eighteen years, done anything reckless. And so I agreed. We eloped that night, but he made me promise to keep it a secret. For the next month we met each weekend. And though he seemed to be growing weaker, he told me he had never been happier. We arranged to meet the following weekend and drive up to his parents' chalet to give them the news. Then, he said, we would tell my family.''

She tried to smile, but even now, after all this time, the pain and humiliation were too deep. ''I suppose it's a story as old as time. Only the names change. And a few minor pieces of the tale. At any rate, this time, when I went to the village inn, he never showed up. I waited all night, certain he would phone. In the morning the phone did ring and I raced to answer it, but it was his mother. She informed me that she and her husband had learned of their son's foolishness and had already taken steps to have the marriage annulled. I asked to speak with JeanClaude, but she informed me that he was too ill to leave his bed. He and his family had known for years that an illness he'd contracted in childhood was terminal. He had, she assured me, done many foolish, reckless things because of it, and his family had understood his need to defy the fates by living life on the edge. It was, she said, simply his way of dealing with the fact that he had so little time. I was nothing more than one more of his messy mistakes that they would have to clean up. But I was young, she told me. I would soon forget. And, she reminded me, I was one of the lucky ones. I had a long and healthy life ahead of me, while her son had, according to his doctors, less than a few weeks left.''

Colin hadn't said a word. Nor had he moved.

But at least, she thought, he hadn't drawn away. Yet.

"There's more, of course. At first I was too ashamed to tell anyone. But then, as the weeks went by, I realized I would have to take my family into my confidence. You see, I realized I was...expecting a baby." She looked up into Colin's eyes. "My family was wonderful. My parents, my sisters, my grandparents formed this loving, protective circle around me. And for the first time I realized just how much they loved me. Without question. Without reservation. All those years of separations, of loneliness, disappeared. We felt this amazing bond as we waited for this new little addition to our family." She touched a hand to her middle, as though, even now, she could feel life growing there. "I wanted the baby so badly. It would be all mine. Just mine. I suppose I was naively thinking that I would make a home with this child. The home I so desperately craved."

She paused a moment, bracing for the pain that she knew would come. Her voice lowered. "But I learned that wanting something with all your heart isn't enough. The doctor said that nature has its own way of removing life's little imperfections." She shook her head, as much in amazement as in denial. "That's what he called it. One of life's little imperfections. And so, less than three months after it all began, it was over. All over."

She couldn't swallow the lump in her throat. To her embarrassment tears welled up in her eyes and spilled down her cheeks.

Mortified, she sniffed. "I never cry."

Before she could turn away, Colin had his arms around her, rocking her like a child. And then the tears became a torrent. Great choking sobs that wracked her body and had her burying her face in his neck.

He pressed his lips to her hair and held her while she cried her heart out.

"Oh, Lizbeth. Oh, baby." His words washed over her, soothing, healing.

He felt the way she struggled to control herself. But the more she tried, the more she wept. A lifetime of tears came spilling out. And with them, a sense of relief that she'd finally unlocked the secrets of her heart. When at last she drew a little away, Colin handed her his handkerchief.

She gave a shaky laugh, that sounded more like a hiccup. "I don't know what's come over me. I haven't cried this hard since that day. I didn't think I had any tears left over it." She took a deep breath. "The doctor counseled me to resume a normal life." She gave a sound that might have been a laugh or a sob. "So I went on to college, and then into the family business, and I never looked back."

"Maybe you should have."

"Why?" Her head came up. "So I can be reminded again how easy it is for all those I love to simply leave me?"

"No, Lizbeth. So you can remember. Remember how it felt to be desperately in love, and anticipating a life together."

"Why should I remember? Why should I invite all that pain again?"

He waited a beat, watching her eyes. "So you'll take pity on me, and understand what I'm feeling."

She went perfectly still. Then she shook her head. "I told you...

"You told me you didn't want any pretty speeches. So I won't make any. I'll just tell you the plain, simple truth, without any sugarcoating. Maybe Serena was right. Maybe you and I are more alike than we know. I've spent a lifetime traveling, and never believing I would find a place where I could stay for more than a few weeks before wanting to move on. I never believed such a place existed. But the minute I met you, I realized I'd found my home and my heart. Maybe you don't want to hear it. But I have to say it anyway. I love you, Lizbeth. Only you. And if you'll have me, I want to marry you, and stay with you, and love you for all of my life."

She looked down at Colin's big workman's hands still holding hers. So strong. So competent. So gentle.

"What if there's a...defect in me? What if I can't ever have a baby?"

He touched a hand to her cheek. "What if I can't? Would it matter to you?"

She huffed out a breath. "Of course not."

"Then I suppose some day we'll find out. But for now, let's just start with each other. And a kitten. And then maybe a puppy. And then..."

He lifted her chin. "I'm sorry. I've made you cry again."

"Yes." She sniffed. "I guess I'm making up for lost time."

"Yeah." He grinned and kissed away the tear that rolled down her cheek. "I hope this isn't going to make you cry even harder." He reached into his pocket and withdrew a small box.

"What's this?"

"Open it, Lizbeth."

She opened the box and saw the glint of a heart-shaped ruby surrounded by glittering diamonds.

"I figured if the kitten didn't win your heart, maybe jewels would do the trick."

"Oh, Colin."

"Will you wear my ring, Lizbeth? Will you marry me, and let me love you forever?"

Her eyes were wide, the tears glistening on her lashes like diamonds. "Yes. Oh, yes."

He slipped the ring on her finger and lifted her hand to his lips.

With a sigh she wrapped her arms around his neck.

Against her lips he whispered, "I hope you don't mind if the whole town knows our secret."

She pulled back. "The whole town?"

He gave her that wonderful grin that never failed to stir her heart. "The Lassiter twins saw me coming out of the jeweler's and hurried inside. I figure by now they've told just about everybody they know."

"Oh, my." She turned away. "We'd better get over to tell Loretta before she hears it from someone else."

He drew her close and covered her mouth with his. "We'll tell her. In a little while. But take pity on me, Lizbeth. I've spent the entire day worrying about whether or not you'd let me past that wall you'd built around your heart. As long as I'm forbidden to make pretty speeches, the least you can do is take me inside and let me show you, in my own clever way, just how much I love you."

"Hmm." She drank in the taste of him, so dark and dangerous and so very, very sweet. "You know, you really can be quite eloquent, even when you don't say a word."

"I was hoping you'd notice." He picked her up and carried her to the door, with the kitten happily weaving around their feet.

Just then the kitten spotted the end of a vine

hanging over the edge of the wheelbarrow and couldn't resist standing up to grab hold. With just one tug the vine pulled away, carrying with it a handful of weeds that scattered over the kitten's head, littering the once clean walkway.

"Looks like she's chosen her own name," Lizbeth said as she surveyed the damage. "Scamp."

"Scamp?" Colin chuckled. "Yeah. I'd say it suits her."

Inside, the clock was just striking the hour. They looked at each other and smiled, remembering Grandpa Sully's words. And found themselves thinking about all the hours of all the days they had to look forward to spending together. Doing nothing more exciting than loving one another for the rest of their lives.

Epilogue

"Lizbeth." Alex stormed into the kitchen of Stafford Cottage and caught her sister's arm. "If you don't come upstairs right this minute and get into your wedding gown, I swear I'll have Grant carry you up."

Alex's handsome new husband stood just behind her. On his face was a delighted grin as he imagined himself carrying the bride to her room like a hostage.

"I'm just seeing to the flowers on the wedding cake."

"I think the chef from our New York hotel is perfectly capable of seeing to the cake." Alex nodded to her sister, Celeste, who caught Lizbeth's other arm. The two forcibly dragged her from the kitchen and up the stairs.

"Now." Once in her bedroom, Alex caught hold of Lizbeth's sweater and tugged it over her head. "Get in that shower. Right this minute. You have a wedding to attend."

"But the food…"

"Is in very good hands. Ditto the flowers. Now move it."

The two sisters shoved her toward the bathroom. Minutes later she emerged from the shower, her hair a mass of wet tangles.

"Sit right here," Alex commanded. "Let's see what we can do with that hair."

"It's hopeless," Lizbeth muttered. "You know it's always had a mind of its own."

"Yeah, well, today we're about to tame the beast." Alex picked up a brush and hair dryer and attacked.

"Speaking of taming the beast…" Celeste began laying out the wedding gown and accessories. "That is one handsome hunk wearing out a path in the parlor carpet."

"He's downstairs?" Lizbeth smiled dreamily. "Pacing?"

"Like a caged panther. It's so sexy." Celeste sighed. "And so…endearing."

When Alex was finished with Lizbeth's hair, the two sisters helped her into her gown and began fastening the row of tiny buttons. Then they stood back to admire their handiwork.

"Oh, Lizbeth." Alex felt a rush of emotion and blamed it on the fact that she'd so recently been through a wedding of her own. "You look so beautiful."

"Yeah." Even Celeste, who considered herself far too sophisticated to cry at weddings, felt a mist of tears. "I don't think you've ever looked prettier. But let's face it. If ever a woman was meant to be a bride, it's you."

"You don't think this is too much?" Lizbeth ran a hand down the beaded bodice, the full, gathered skirt of raw silk, fit for a princess.

"On you it's perfect." Celeste, whose taste was impeccable, spoke with confidence. "And you're perfect, too, Beth."

Lizbeth kissed both her sisters' cheeks.

At a knock on the door they looked up to find their parents and grandfather eager to see the bride. They had spent the past week in Stafford, meeting Colin and his sister and brother-in-law, who had flown in from Fiji, and getting acquainted with all Lizbeth's friends and neighbors. There was a flurry of tears and laughter, and fierce embraces all around.

Her grandfather shook his head in wonder. "It's hard to believe my little LizzyBeth is getting married." He caught her hands in his and stared into her eyes. "You must have made quite an impression on the people of Stafford. Do you realize the entire town is downstairs, milling around the parlor and spilling out into your garden?''

''Yes.'' Lizbeth's eyes were shining. ''Isn't it wonderful?''

''It is indeed.'' He winked at the others. ''I'd say you've acquired quite an extended family here in Stafford.''

''I guess I hadn't thought about it quite that way, but you're right, Grandpa Sully. They are like family. Every one of them.''

They looked up when Loretta, cane in hand, paused in the doorway. Lizbeth hurried over to lead her inside. She indicated a chair and Loretta sank down gratefully.

Lizbeth knelt in front of her and held out a small jeweler's box.

''What's this?'' The old woman glanced from the box to Lizbeth's wide smile.

''Colin and I wanted you to have this.''

The old woman opened the box. Inside was a lovely double strand of pearls with a jeweled clasp. ''Oh.'' Her eyes were shining. ''This is far too grand.''

''We'd like you to wear it.'' Lizbeth fastened it around Loretta's neck. ''And, since you're the closest thing we have to a grandmother, we'd like you to sit with our family during the ceremony.'' She kissed the old woman's cheek. ''Especially since you had a hand in getting us together.''

"Speaking of the ceremony…" Celeste, determined to keep everything to a schedule, glanced at her watch. "I'm told that Reverend Watson and his wife are here, and waiting to begin."

Lizbeth's parents kissed their daughter before leaving. Then her two sisters did the same. Loretta got slowly to her feet and pressed a kiss to Lizbeth's cheek. Patrick Sullivan gathered his granddaughter close for a quick, hard hug. Then he and Loretta walked out together, looking extremely pleased with themselves. It occurred to Lizbeth that those two old connivers looked awfully chummy. Almost as if they'd known from the beginning just how this would end. Could they have planned such a thing? After all, Colin had been to Lake Como, studying architecture. And Grandpa Sully was almost as sly as Loretta.

She quickly dismissed such a thought.

Hearing the music start, she took a deep breath and started toward the door. Just then she looked up to see Colin in the doorway, his eyes hot and fierce as he studied her. His look softened as he stepped closer, keeping one hand behind his back.

Lizbeth smiled. "Getting nervous?"

"I was. But not now." He touched a finger to her cheek. "You look like one of those beautiful creatures in a fairytale."

"That's how I feel. As if none of this could possibly be real." She studied the way he looked, so tall, so ruggedly handsome in his dark tuxedo.

"I'm almost afraid to touch you, for fear you'll disappear."

"I'm not going anywhere, Lizbeth." He lifted her hand to his lips. "I've waited too long, worked too hard for this. You're stuck with me for the rest of your life."

"Promise?"

He nodded. "That's what we're about to do down there. In front of the entire town of Stafford." He brought his other hand from behind his back to reveal the most stunning bouquet of garden flowers, fabulous white roses and lilies and babies' breath, tied with lace, and trailing delicate strands of ivy. "I thought, since you talk to them so much, they ought to be part of this."

"Oh, Colin." She buried her face in them and blinked back a tear.

Hearing the music swell, he caught her hand, linking his fingers with hers. "We'd better get down there before your sister Celeste comes looking for us. Did you know she's asked to be the first guest on Serena and Gary's new boat?"

"I'm not surprised. Wanderlust is big in our family."

"Was," he corrected. "We're about to change all that."

As they descended the stairs, Lizbeth caught sight of the Lassiter twins in neon pink gowns with matching parasols. Alfreda was holding Scamp, while Winifred was blinking back tears.

As she and Colin made their way toward the minister, standing in the middle of the garden, they passed Bill and Sue Yardley, who waved. Seth Simpson was smiling broadly. Amy Mullins and Vicky Carter were whispering behind their hands. Jack Nowack and his wife stood holding their daughter's hands and beaming at the happy couple.

Lizbeth's nerves dissolved, replaced with the most wonderful feeling of serenity. She was meant to be here. In this place. With this man. Pledging her love for all eternity.

Home, she thought. She'd made a wonderful place for herself here in this close-knit, loving community. But it was Colin's love that had finally, ultimately, made it home. For home wasn't just a place. She knew now that home was really a feeling deep in the heart. And her heart was nearly filled to bursting with love for this man. Wherever Colin was, that would be her home. For now. For always. Forever.

* * * * *

Read about the youngest
Sullivan sister in

SEDUCING CELESTE

coming next month
only in

Silhouette Intimate Moments

LINDSAY McKENNA

continues her most popular series with a
brand-new, longer-length book.

And it's the story you've been waiting for....

Morgan's Mercenaries:
Heart of Stone

They had met before. Battled before. And
Captain Maya Stevenson had never again
wanted to lay eyes on Major Dane York—
the man who once tried to destroy
her military career! But on their latest
mission together, Maya discovered that beneath
the fury in Dane's eyes lay a raging passion. Now she
struggled against dangerous desire, as Dane's command
over her seemed greater still. For this time, he laid claim
to her heart....

Only from Lindsay McKenna and Silhouette Books!

"When it comes to action and romance,
nobody does it better than Ms. McKenna."
—*Romantic Times Magazine*

Available in March at your favorite retail outlet.

Silhouette®
Where love comes alive™

Visit Silhouette at www.eHarlequin.com   PSMMHO

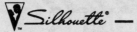

Silhouette® —

where love comes alive—online...

eHARLEQUIN.com

your romantic escapes

—Indulgences—

♥ Monthly guides to indulging yourself, such as:
  ★ Tub Time: A guide for bathing beauties
  ★ Magic Massages: A treat for tired feet

—Horoscopes—

♥ Find your daily Passionscope, weekly Lovescopes and Erotiscopes

♥ Try our compatibility game

—Reel Love—

♥ Read all the latest romantic movie reviews

—Royal Romance—

♥ Get the latest scoop on your favorite royal romances

—Romantic Travel—

♥ For the most romantic destinations, hotels and travel activities

SINTE1

Every mother wants to see her children marry
and have little ones of their own.

One mother decided to take matters into
her own hands....

Now three Texas-born brothers are about to discover
that mother knows best: A strong man *does* need a
good woman. And babies make a forever family!

Matters of the Heart

A Mother's Day collection of
three **brand-new** stories by

Pamela Morsi
Ann Major
Annette Broadrick

Available in April at your favorite retail outlets,
only from Silhouette Books!

Where love comes alive™

#1 *New York Times* bestselling author

NORA ROBERTS

brings you more of the loyal and loving,
tempestuous and tantalizing Stanislaski family.

Coming in February 2001

The Stanislaski Sisters

Natasha and Rachel

Though raised in the Old World traditions of their
family, fiery Natasha Stanislaski and cool, classy
Rachel Stanislaski are ready for a *new* world of love...

And also available in February 2001 from
Silhouette Special Edition, the newest book in the
heartwarming Stanislaski saga

CONSIDERING KATE

Natasha and Spencer Kimball's daughter Kate turns her
back on old dreams and returns to her hometown, where
she finds the *man* of her dreams.

Available at your favorite retail outlet.

Where love comes alive™

Visit Silhouette at www.eHarlequin.com